Chuga the Beluga

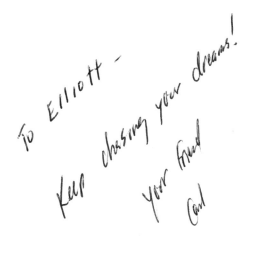

To Elliott –
Keep chasing your dreams!
Your friend
Carl

aug 2015

Chuga the Beluga

written by: Carl F. Kristeller
illustrations by: Joshua Anthony Sacco

ISBN: 1512116351
ISBN 13: 9781512116359
Library of Congress Control Number: 2015907952
CreateSpace Independent Publishing Platform,
North Charleston, South Carolina

This book is dedicated to Wink
For always loving us, and believing
in us, no matter what. Thanks Mom!

1

"Chuga," called Jenuga once, and then again with more urgency and conviction in her voice. "Chuuuuuuga! Come on baby, it's time to go."

Jenuga knew they could wait no longer. It was a long trip and would take most of the next month to complete. It was always a dangerous trip going north, but this year could be worse as it was just the two of them. Two weeks earlier, they'd waved goodbye to their close friends and family as even they could wait no longer for Jenuga and Chuga to start the journey. Chuga was just too small and weak to make the trip.

He'd been born in a timely fashion, but was alarmingly small and slow to gain strength. It was not his fault. It was nobody's fault. It's just the way it was. Jenuga was just happy Chuga survived. Jenuga's closest friend

Finuga had helped her as much as she could, but her mate Kruga – the leader of their small pod – had been anxious to leave. Time was short. The safety of the pod depended on their timely departure. Everyone knew Kruga was right, and Finuga soon joined him as the pod said their goodbyes, leaving Jenuga and Chuga behind.

After two short weeks of nursing and exercising, Chuga seemed ready and Jenuga knew it was time to go. She hoped that by leaving later they could avoid the usual dangers of the annual trek, although making the trip without the protection of their small pod could also be very dangerous. Many a year passed where those who lagged behind due to age or weakness were never seen again.

Jenuga remained confident because Chuga had developed great energy and quickness, if not the normal size and lasting strength of a young white whale. She knew she must be ever watchful during the long journey and keep her diminutive son close at all times.

Chuga was playing with a small shell nearby when he heard Mama's first call. He continued to push the shell along until he heard her call again in her 'do it now' voice. He quickly dropped the shell and rushed to her side.

"Here I am Mama," said Chuga.

"There you are," she said, "come along now baby, it's time to go!"

Oh boy, thought Chuga. He'd been waiting for this day ever since Mama told him about the trip they would take. He was so excited! He could barely remember the others before they left. He hadn't been able to play with them because of his lack of endurance. He'd been forced to stay with Mama and spent most of his time learning to swim, breathe, and feed while being supported on her back. When the others left he could tell it made Mama sad, and he knew it was because of him. He didn't like it when Mama was sad. So he worked as hard as he could, and though he hadn't grown much, he grew stronger each day and learned a lot from listening to Mama's stories.

As they started north, Chuga swam playfully around and around Mama. He was full of joy and anticipation. "Mama," said Chuga, "tell me again where we're going." Mama had told him many times, but he never tired of hearing about it.

"We're going to the Black Pebbled Beach in the Northern Sea," said Mama, "where we'll meet up with all our friends and family."

"And there will be lots of other kids for me to play with, right Mama?" he asked, already knowing the answer.

"Yes," said Mama playing along, "lots and lots."

"How long before we get there?"

"It's a long journey so save your energy and stop racing around!"

"Okay Mama," he said. Chuga knew he should listen to Mama and do as she said. She knew so much about everything and there was a lot to learn. He swam up close to her side and glided along beside her, settling in for the long journey.

2

In a cold dark cave, hidden under the snow covered hills of the north, the White Beast stirred. He rolled from his left side to his back, slowly stretched his full length, yawned, then flopped onto his right side. He snorted loudly, snuggled his muzzle into his large paws, and eased back into a restless slumber. He was running out of time. He could sense the change in seasons outside his winter's den, and feel the stirrings of hunger in his empty, shrunken belly.

3

J enuga and Chuga had been swimming for days
now and there were many exciting things to see.
There were many different kinds of creatures swimming in the cool waters of the big wide ocean. Chuga
wanted to explore and play with all of them, and now
and then Mama would allow it while they took time
to rest from their journey. Mostly Mama wanted to
keep going and she warned Chuga to stay close by
her side. She told him stories about all the different
creatures. She told him where they lived, what they
ate, if they were friendly or not, and what they were
called.

She talked about the dangers in the sea and how to
avoid them by fleeing or hiding. She told him about the
Orcas of the sea and the Polar Bears of the land. The

Black Beasts and the White Beasts. They had not seen the land of the White Beasts yet so she mostly talked about the Black Beasts. She described how they hunted in packs and would eat them if they could. She warned that they must be avoided at all costs, and if you saw them it may already be too late. She taught Chuga to recognize the signs that could mean they were close and what to do if he saw any of those signs. She sternly warned him about hesitating or taking the signs lightly. She hated scaring Chuga, but knew it could save his life one day. She knew he must learn these lessons because she would not be able to protect him at all times. So they practiced hiding in the rocks and diving down deep along the sea floor. They practiced scanning the horizon from the surface and the shallows from the depths.

One day they came upon a small island and Chuga was amazed to see the sea floor rise above the water's surface. Mama had told him about the land, but this was his first time seeing it. Even more amazing were the creatures that moved about upon the land. "They're people," said Mama, "and they live on the land. Sometimes they come into the water, but they don't go far from the land because they're not good swimmers. Mostly they use floating machines called ships and boats and race around making loud noises and churning up the sea. And Chuga," she continued, "it's very important you stay as far away from them as you can because they will hunt you for food just like the White and Black Beasts I told you about. You must stay clear of the land whenever possible because you cannot walk like they do. It is very dangerous."

"Why?" asked Chuga.

"Because," said Mama, "if you get too close the tide can push you onto the land where you can get stranded. We are swimmers and cannot survive on the land."

"How can they survive?"

"I don't know. Like all the creatures of the sea are different, and can do different things, there are just as many that live on land. Like the birds in the air that fly on the wind, we can't understand all the ways of the world, but we can learn from them and keep ourselves safe."

"Okay," said Chuga. He knew Mama must be right. She knew so many things and he was eager to learn as much as possible. Sometimes Chuga would get scared by the things Mama told him, but he knew it was important.

Mama would hug Chuga when she saw he was scared, but she would always stress the seriousness of the lessons he must learn. 'It's good to be afraid,' she'd say, 'if it will keep you safe!'

4

Each new day brought new curiosities and adventures for Chuga. The environment continued to change with each mile they traveled. They saw new lands with mountains that got lost in the clouds, and others that barely showed above the surface. There were big islands that went on forever, filled with the land dwelling creatures and the homes they built. There were boats and ships that filled the rivers and inlets that flowed into the sea, and others that ventured far from the land. There were those that rested upon the sea floor, never to drift among the waves again. Ships both big and small, abandoned by the people who built them, and now home to the many plant-like animals of the ocean and their neighboring fishes, crabs and the like.

There were small islands where only the birds dotted the sand and rocks. They would fly out over the sea and dive straight down into the water to catch the small fish that made the mistake of swimming too close to the surface. There were other birds that dove down and seemed to fly through the water chasing the deeper swimming fish. They would dart around only to return to the surface, spread their wings, and rise back into the wind and sky.

The birds fascinated Chuga. He watched them fly about, high above the sea or hovering just above the ocean swells. He wondered what it would be like to fly. They could hang in the sky all day with their wings spread wide, and many times he saw them far from any land, riding the wind in search of food. To see the world from those great heights filled Chuga's dreams with sights only his imagination could guess.

There was a day when a large group of dolphins raced by heading somewhere in a big hurry. They leaped high in the air, trying to fly, only to splash down and race on. They flipped and twisted in the air and sea, seemingly showing off their acrobatic skills for Mama and Chuga as they passed. Mama grew concerned about the playful dolphins because she knew they could hurt Chuga because of his small size. She made him stay close to her side. She was too big for them to bother with, but there were so many of them, she was relieved to see they were more interested in where they were going than anything else. Her relief faded quickly when she began wondering where they were headed in such a hurry. There may be something ahead that could attract some of the sea's larger predators. The ones in particular she worried about were the largest of the dolphins, the Black Beasts. After the dolphins had passed she led Chuga to a small inlet with a white sand beach and explained her fears to him as they rested a while.

While they rested, they found some strange crafts on the sea floor which Mama explained were called planes and were used by the people to fly through the air. When Chuga asked when they would leave the water and fly again, Mama guessed they wouldn't. She said they'd been there for many years and were like the abandoned shells left behind by the sand crabs and other small creatures. When he asked where they came from she showed him the straight white lines streaming across the sky, and the shiny specks that raced ahead. They were much higher than even the highest birds. Chuga wished he could be up there to see the world from such a height. He so wished he could fly.

He swam around the flying machines that sat on the sea bottom and studied their wings and tailfins, which were much like his own. He thought about how sad it was they would never fly again. He remembered the sunken ships and realized there were many machines that couldn't or wouldn't ever float or fly again. It made him happy to know he could swim around so freely. He didn't need machines to enjoy the world around him. Although he would always wish he could fly, he really liked being able to dart around in the sea.

Another day they came upon a large Blue Whale and her newborn calf. Chuga couldn't believe the size of them. They were bigger than anything he'd ever seen. The calf was bigger than Mama, and when she told him it was probably only as old as he was, he couldn't believe it. Mama allowed Chuga to slow their pace as he matched the Blue Whale's speed, and they swam along with them for a while. Chuga listened to their songs and tried to sing along with them. He was awed by their power and grace as they seemed to glide effortlessly through the water.

A few days later Chuga surprised a school of strange looking fish and playfully chased after them. He was delighted to see them launch themselves up out of the water, spread their oversize flippers, and sail just above the waves for long stretches before diving back into the water, only to launch themselves again. Chuga was amazed to see the fish fly. He tried to launch himself as they had, and the dolphins he remembered from before. Because he was so small, he was able to propel most of himself above the surface, but when he spread his flippers to fly he would only crash down on his belly splashing water in all directions. As hard as he tried he could not free himself of the water's grip, and Mama chuckled at his repeated attempts.

When Chuga asked Mama why he couldn't fly her response was the same as with all things she couldn't fully explain. 'There are many different kinds of creatures in this world. Whales are not meant to fly,' she'd say, 'birds fly, whales and fishes swim, crabs, lobsters and people walk. It seems we must always be moving to survive, and all creatures do this in their own way. It is not always for us to know how or why, but to make the best of our own abilities.' Chuga knew Mama was right, but it didn't stop him from dreaming about flying and how free it must feel.

As the days passed, and the adventures continued, Chuga learned many things. Mama taught him all she could. He was very curious. He was always asking questions and exploring everything Mama would allow him to.

There were days and nights of stormy seas where the wind whipped and howled and kicked the waves up into mountainous swells of crashing foam. Lightning would flash from the dark, angry clouds while the stinging rains beat down on the surface above. Those days they swam through the depths to avoid the turbulent seas, coming up only when necessary to catch a breath and dive again. Chuga would be bounced around mercilessly in these rough waters and tired easily.

Then there were days when the sea was flat and calm and they could swim along the surface. Though clouds would come and go, most days they swam under the warm, blue, sunny skies, and most nights under the moon and a blanket of stars. They watched the moon in the night sky grow smaller with each passing night till it was just a sliver in the sky, and then begin to grow to its full round again like the Sand Dollar. Mama talked about the Black Pebbled Beach and told Chuga about the sun that would shine for most of the day, and how the moon and stars would only visit the sky for a short period of time.

Whenever Mama talked about the Black Pebbled Beach, Chuga noticed how sad she got. She missed her friends and he knew how important they were. He couldn't wait to get there and make some friends of his own. He wondered what they would be like. He often wanted to stop and make friends with those he met along the way, but Mama usually wanted to push on, promising again and again that he would make many new friends when they reached their destination.

Mama was the best. She was his teacher, his protector, and his friend. He loved her very much. He loved to hear the stories she told about all she knew. He didn't like when she was sad, so whenever she asked him to keep going he always tried to follow along without question. He knew how happy she would be when they reached the Black Pebbled Beach. He understood the importance of their journey.

5

The White Beast lay motionless, fighting the urge that drew him from his slumber. He stretched his limbs, blinked open his eyes, and looked about the cool den that had served him so well during his long winter's nap. The outside light seeped in from the snow-covered mouth of the cave. He rolled to his uneasy stomach and dragged himself toward the faint light. It was time to go. He scratched and clawed at the hardened snow with his strong paws. He broke through and poked his head out the small opening he'd created. He took a deep breath of the clean, crisp, cold air he found. He quickly busted open a larger hole and pulled his massive body through the opening. He allowed himself to slide down the side of the steep hill below his cave, stood up, and shook off the remaining slumber of his long hibernation.

The White Beast put his nose to the air but found nothing of note. He looked north at the mountains that rose majestically to the cloud covered sky. He looked south at the long snow-blanketed valley laid out before him. He took a last look up the hill at the den he would abandon. His stomach growled weakly as he thought of the plentiful sea beyond the valley floor. The sound of rushing water hidden under the snow and ice nearby set him to motion. He turned down the valley and ambled off, carrying his hunger with him.

6

Early one morning, as they traveled along with the sun shining down from a clear blue sky, Jenuga thought she heard a new sound. It was a sound she'd heard before and was well aware of what it could be. She listened intently until there was no doubt. It frightened her. Up ahead, in their intended path were the faint sounds of panic and dismay. The unmistakable sounds of danger.

"Chuga," Mama called, "come here baby." Chuga heard Mama but was busy swimming along with a sea turtle and did not respond.

"Chuga!" barked Mama in her 'do it now' voice. "Come here now!" Chuga reluctantly waved the turtle goodbye and swam slowly to Mama's side. "When I call you," she scolded, "you come right away! I think there's danger nearby so we must take cover!"

Mama crested the surface with Chuga in tow. She looked skyward and scanned the horizon. She watched the seabirds race past in large numbers. They'd seen many seabirds along the way, but not this many moving this fast in one direction. Coupled with the sounds of distress it confirmed Mama's suspicions. It was another telltale sign of the danger ahead. She gathered up Chuga and slowed their progress. She quickly instructed Chuga in the immediate sights and sounds and explained their meaning. When Chuga did not respond with the urgency she felt, she hissed "Chuga!" and waited to catch his eye. This time Chuga caught her urgency and looked directly at Mama.

"Take a deep breath and get ready," she said. She now had his full attention. She'd taught him how to hide in the rocks or dive deep when necessary to avoid such dangers. She scanned the sky again and said, "we're going to dive down and look around. Something's wrong, do you understand?" Her tone left no doubt in Chuga's mind and he nodded his head and filled his lungs with air.

"Ok, let's go," instructed Mama and she shoved Chuga downward following fast in his wake.

They dove down about fifty feet and Mama led them out of the swift ocean current and into calmer waters. Chuga hugged close to her side and watched as she tuned into the surrounding sea with all her senses. They swam slowly and cautiously on, both on high alert. After a few tense moments, Mama was about to lead them up for air when she stopped dead still and held Chuga back. She searched the surrounding waters for the presence of the predator she felt but had not yet seen. Looking up she saw a large, dark shadow pass above them gliding slowly.

The Black Beast slid effortlessly through the water but hadn't seemed to notice them yet. Mama gestured to Chuga and whispered forcefully, "Come on baby, stay with Mama. We're going to dive!" and down they went. She took them to the ocean's floor where she could keep a close watch above without worrying about the depths below. With Chuga tight to her side they quickly reached the bottom. They would need to get some air soon, but she wasn't worried about that yet. She saw the sea floor rise in one direction and knew if they could reach the shallow waters the Black Beasts would not be able to reach them. She recognized these waters and knew them well. Her family had passed this way for many years on their annual treks north and south.

Mama led Chuga up the gently sloping bottom as it slowly rose toward land and the water's surface. They scurried along the bottom as more shadows passed quickly above. Again, they didn't seem to be noticed due to the beasts' preoccupation with what lay ahead. With Chuga following closely, Mama led them as they weaved in and out of the coral reefs that protected the land ahead and heard the waves crashing above. Mama soon found the narrow gap in the craggy rocks that hid the welcomed cove she sought. She had visited it before and they had little trouble sneaking in.

The rocks – hard and jagged – formed a seawall that kept the large predators at bay and provided a safe haven for those small enough to pass. There was danger here also, for at the same time they'd eventually have to leave, and those same predators could be waiting for them. They could never underestimate the intelligence and patience of those hunters. They were hungry too!

For now, out of immediate danger, they could rest. They were in the small, protective, clam shaped cove of the Pink Sand Beach. It would provide shelter and the food they needed before continuing on their journey. It was a good time for Mama to show Chuga some of the things she'd only been able to tell him about before. She pointed out the seabirds in the distance and explained again how they followed the Black Beasts and fed on their scraps. Chuga, who was still scared and on full alert, paid close attention. He understood the importance of all Mama's lessons and was able to see this one first hand. He never wanted to see those dark shadows that frightened him so much again.

Mama had saved them from the Black Beasts with her quick reactions. She was smart. She knew a lot, and Chuga knew because of his small size he would have to learn to outthink and outwit his many foes to survive. He asked a lot of questions and listened intently to Mama's responses. He learned quickly and well. His fright taught him not to take these lessons lightly and it was good they had this experience, and the time to discuss it together. They had traveled far, but they were not there yet. They were getting closer and closer to their destination, but still had a long way to go, and the possibility of more danger ahead. Mama kept a watchful eye to the sea and sky, monitoring the nearby danger. She wanted to wait till long after the area was clear before moving on. She was relieved to escape the close encounter with the Black Beasts, and happy for the lesson it taught Chuga. She was pleased that he seemed to understand the importance of the lessons and was certain he would not soon forget what he'd seen.

As the sun neared its midday peak in the blue sky, Mama and Chuga got visitors.

7

Mama was still not ready to leave when a small family of people appeared from the trees onto the beach. They were caught by surprise and Mama barely managed to lead Chuga to a hiding spot in the nearby rocks. They were not noticed and watched in fascination as the people groomed the beach to their liking and settled in.

"Stay quiet baby," said Mama, "we can't let them see us."

"Why not?" asked Chuga, unable to look away. He craned his neck around the rocks to see better.

"If they see us we'll have to leave," she answered while pulling him down lower in the water.

"Why Mama?" he asked again. "What are they?"

"Well," began Mama, "they're some of the people I told you about. And they can be just as dangerous as the Black Beasts. I've heard some of our friends say they were nice to them and others tell of how they chased them in their boats trying to stab them with long spears. It's best just to avoid them altogether because you don't know which is which. Just like all the creatures of the sea, it's better to be safe than sorry."

"They don't look dangerous. Can we stay and watch them?"

"I'm afraid we'll have to for now. There is certain danger out there still." Mama turned to look beyond the rocks to the open sea. "But you must stay quiet and not let them see us or we may have to go no matter what."

"How come Mama?"

"Because if they see us they may not let us be. They are as curious of us as you seem to be of them, and could try to catch or harm us. We are very different from them and even if they are nice we should not let our guard down around them."

"Okay, Mama," said Chuga remembering her many lessons and their importance. So they settled in to quietly watch the strangers.

There were three of them and Mama explained which one was the Mommy, which was the Daddy, and the little one who looked like the Mommy with her long hair. She was about the same size as Chuga and he watched her most of all. Mama and Chuga watched them flop around in the calm shallow water close to the land's edge. They ran in and out of the water jumping and splashing about. They threw a ball around and the Daddy chased it when it drifted away. Chuga wanted to join them in their fun. As they laughed and played he was fascinated by the little one and barely noticed the time go by. He stayed quiet and still so he couldn't be seen. He didn't want to have to leave.

When the people seemed to tire they returned to the beach to eat. Then they played in the pink sand building tall castles using water they carried onto the beach in small buckets. Later, the Daddy inflated a floating island and the little one carried it to the water. She climbed on top and started to paddle around.

"Stay close to the beach," called the Mommy, "so the tide doesn't carry you away." She watched as the small waves pulled back the water exposing more of the pink sand below.

"Okay Mommy," said the little one and she settled down on the floating island gently riding the small waves up and down. The Mommy and Daddy relaxed on the beach while keeping a watchful eye on the little one.

Mama also noticed the shift in the tide. Soon the water would grow shallow around her and Chuga as it slowly drained from the small cove. There would still be plenty of water to move about in, and she knew it posed them no danger. They would still be able to leave the cove easily even at low tide. The large craggy rocks that sheltered the cove also worked to soften the rolling waves that accompanied the receding tide. The bottom dropped off quickly and there was plenty of room to sneak out through the narrow gap if seen. They hadn't been seen and there was no reason to leave yet. Chuga was being good by her side and seemed hypnotized by the people. Especially the little one. It was a good lesson for him to watch them and learn, so she felt no need to worry.

It was quiet for a short while as they all comfortably passed the time. They let their guard down. The tide continued to vacate the small cove and Mama was the first to notice the water slowly pulling the sleepy little one away from the shoreline and carry her towards the jagged rocks.

Chuga felt the tension grow in Mama's side and knew something was wrong. He looked around swiftly but saw nothing. When he looked at Mama he followed her stare to the little one on the floating island. He'd been watching her so closely he failed to see the danger she was headed for. Mama gasped as the little one was carried by the ebbing tide closer and closer to the jagged rocks. Chuga cried out in alarm!

Suddenly there was a loud commotion on the beach as the Mommy and Daddy recognized the danger. The Mommy yelled to the little one with fear in her voice! The Daddy jumped up, raced into the water, swimming frantically in her direction.

The little one awoke from the noise, saw the rocks only a few feet away, and tried to propel the floating island back to shore. But the tide was too strong and continued to drag her towards the jagged rocks.

Mama, Chuga, and the Mommy all realized in the same instant that the Daddy wasn't going to make it in time. He was still too far away. Before Mama could stop him, Chuga dashed out from the rocks and raced to the little one. He squeezed himself between her and the rocks and gently nudged her floating island away from the jagged rocks and back towards the beach. The little one hung on for dear life. She called in fright to her Mommy and Daddy. Mama raced to corral Chuga just as they reached the Daddy. He grabbed the floating island and dragged it the rest of the way to the beach. Chuga was stubborn and refused to stop helping until they were close to shore.

The Daddy scooped up the little one in his arms and carried her onto the pink sand, into the awaiting arms of the frantic Mommy. "Are you okay, Lilly?" she asked. Her fear gripped her still as she inspected the little one for injury and found none. She hugged the scared little one close as the Daddy pulled the floating island from the surf.

"I'm okay, Mommy," she said, allowing herself to be fawned over, "thanks to that dolphin."

They turned and looked at the white whales in the water. They knew the small white whale had probably saved her life and they stared in disbelief.

Chuga stared back at the little one surprised at himself at how close he'd come to her. Mama swam in and tried to direct him away from the shore. Chuga easily slipped her efforts and eased closer, unable to take his eyes off the little one. Mama had to move back to the deeper water and all she could do was watch. Chuga danced and smiled and wagged his head at the little one.

"Look Mommy," said the little one. "That's a funny looking dolphin." She had already forgotten about the jagged rocks.

The Mommy was the first to find her voice and said, "I don't think it's a dolphin. See the white color? I think it's a Beluga Whale."

"I think you're right," said the Daddy, "they're known as the canaries of the sea due to their wide range of vocalizations and constant singing." He watched with them as the small Beluga Whale danced about and returned to stare at them from a few feet away. "He seems to like us," he added without thinking.

"He's so small. I thought whales were much bigger," said the little one. She clung to the Mommy's neck, unable to take her eyes off the little white whale.

"There are many different kinds of creatures in the sea, Lilly," said the Daddy, "and many different types of whales too, some big and some small."

"True," said the Mommy, "there are so many amazing animals in the sea that we almost never see. I can't believe he's so close. It looks like he wants to play."

Chuga splashed around and once again wagged his head. "I'm Chuga!" he said to the little one and she laughed. "Chuga!" he said again and watched her try to repeat the sound.

"What's that he's saying?" asked the Mommy.

"Shoooga," tried the little one and giggled as the small white whale seemed to dance with glee!

Chuga rolled to his back, slapped his flippers on his belly, and cried again, "Chuga!"

"Chooga!" exclaimed the little one in triumph, and watched him roll and splash in excitement. "It must be his name! It's Chuga the Beluga, Mommy!," she blurted out. "Hi Chuga! I'm Lilly!" she cried, pointing to herself.

"Elilleee," he tried to repeat. Chuga remembered how they'd yelled that to her. He knew it was her name. He tried again to get it right. "Lilleee," he said with more success.

"That's right! I'm Lilly!" She continued to point at herself. "And you're Chuga," she said pointing now at him as she repeated his name.

"Lilly, Lilly, Lilly," repeated Chuga over and over as he danced about in the shallow water, being careful not to get too close to the land.

Mama had drifted back into deeper water and watched in fear and wonder as the two little kids seemed to understand each other.

The Mommy and Daddy were unable to look away as they too were surprised by the apparent understanding the two children shared.

"Can I play with him, Mommy. Please Mommy?"

"Ohh, I don't know Lilly. It could be dangerous. He is a wild animal you know."

"But look Mommy, he's just a little kid like me. He's not even big enough to hurt me even if he wanted to. And look, that must be his mommy over there." She pointed at the larger white whale floating a short distance away.

Mommy looked at the larger Beluga whale and saw the love and concern in a mother's eyes. Their eyes met and a warm comfort passed over her.

Mama, without knowing why, nodded slowly and backed a little further away. She felt a sudden kinship she could not explain and knew it would be all right. These were some of the nice ones.

"Nothing's going to happen," pleaded Lilly, trying to reassure her Mommy. "Look at him. He likes me. He just wants to play. He wants to be my friend."

Chuga couldn't contain himself and danced about joyfully. He looked at Mama and was overjoyed when she told him to be careful.

"Okay," said Mommy, then added quickly, "but wait," as Lilly tried to free herself from Mommy's arms. "Only if you hold Daddy's hand and stay close to his side," she continued and greeted the shocked questioning look the Daddy sent her. "Look at them," she said in response, "they're just kids who want to play together. There can't be any harm in that. Look how small he is. Just stand out there with her for a few minutes and see what happens. If it doesn't feel right then come back in."

Daddy reached out and took Lilly's hand with a firm squeeze as Mommy gently placed her on the soft pink sand. He leaned down and in a firm voice said to Lilly. "You heard Mommy, stay close and don't let go of my hand."

"Okay," came her reply as they waded slowly into the calm, shallow water where Chuga waited gleefully.

Chuga settled long enough to shout "Lilly!" before spinning around with a small splash of his flipper.

Lilly giggled and reached with her free hand to splash Chuga back. Chuga spun again and this time threw more water their way with a flick of his tailfin.

Now even Daddy joined in, splashing small handfuls of water in Chuga's direction. Chuga belly-flopped in delight, sending more spray at Lilly and her Daddy. Daddy dropped Lilly's hand and playfully used both hands to drench Chuga while encouraging Lilly to do the same.

Soon they were all laughing and splashing about when Lilly stopped and held out her hand, just above the water's surface. Chuga advanced slowly to Lilly's outstretched hand and welcomed her gentle touch. She rubbed his bulbous head in short smooth strokes. Chuga rolled to his back to show her his belly. She stroked his belly like she would a small puppy.

Lilly looked at Daddy and he nodded his consent then added quickly, "You stay right here close to the beach. You don't go any deeper than your belly button or out you'll come." He stayed in the water to watch from close by.

"Okay," came Lilly's reply as she joined Chuga in playful fun.

They made fast friends as they played together for the next hour or so. They splashed and laughed and swam about in the shallow water. Chuga chased and retrieved the small ball Lilly threw and flipped it back to her. He pulled her gently back and forth on his back as she hung on tight to his flippers, mindful not to stray too far from the shore. They played catch and tag and chatted up a storm.

Daddy joined Mommy on the pink sand at the water's edge and they watched with amazement. Neither could help smiling and laughing as the new friends frolicked and played together.

Mama smiled and relaxed a little as she watched from the deeper water.

After a while, as the sun moved across the afternoon sky and began its descent, Mommy called out "Come on Lilly, time's up. It's going to get dark soon so it's time to go."

"Just a few more minutes, please, Mommy?"

"You can have five minutes to say goodbye to your friend, but then we must go."

"Thank you, Mommy."

Mommy and Daddy walked up the beach and started packing up their stuff.

"I have to go," Lilly said sadly to Chuga and he understood without protest. He knew the importance of moving on when the time came. They hugged as long as they could and promised to see each other again some-day. Then Lilly leaned down and kissed Chuga on the head and stroked his back one last time before reluc-tantly turning and walking away.

Chuga watched as Lilly slowly walked from the wa-ter and into her Mommy's awaiting arms. Her Mommy dried Lilly off and tucked her into a warm towel as she shivered in the cooling breeze. Her Daddy lifted their things and together they trudged up the soft pink sand to the edge of the trees. With a last wave to Chuga, Lilly turned and raced down the path and out of sight.

8

The blue sky melted into the blue of the calm sea and only the shimmer on the farthest reaches of the horizon gave any clue to the meeting of the two very different worlds. Mama watched the colors fade into the gathering dusk as Chuga stared at the empty Pink Sand Beach, both heartbreak and joy fighting for his attention. He was as happy as he was sad. Happy for the new friend he'd made, and sad to see her go, not knowing when he would see her again. When her Mommy called him Lilly's friend they had smiled at each other and the bond they were forging was cemented. He knew he would see her again.

The seabirds had long since disappeared from the distant sky and Mama knew they too would have to leave soon. It looked safe. There were no more sounds of distress in the gentle sea. Mama decided to wait for dark and allow Chuga time to reconcile himself before moving on.

When it was time, Mama called Chuga to her side and with her saddened baby in tow, they cautiously slipped through the jagged rocks and back to the open sea. Through the cover of darkness they rejoined the northern currents and were carried along on their journey.

Chuga remained quiet most of the night – deep in thought – until the morning sun shone down and seemed to lift his spirits. As they swam along he started, and then couldn't stop, talking about his new friend Lilly. He told Mama about all the fun they had and she nodded with a knowing smile. When he told Mama he couldn't wait to tell all the new friends he'd make about her, she stopped him in his wake.

"You mustn't tell anyone about Lilly, baby," she stated sadly.

"Why not, Mama?" he asked as his heart sank. "She's my friend."

"I know, baby, and it's great that you made a friend, but you remember what I told you about people? Some are nice like Lilly and her family, but some are not. Some people want to capture and harm us like the Black Beasts. If you tell your new friends about them, and how nice they were, then they might think all people are nice and not be afraid of them. If they're not afraid they could get hurt or worse by the people who aren't nice."

"Worse?" questioned Chuga.

"Yes, baby. Much worse. Some humans hunt us for food. You don't want your friends to be hunted do you?"

"No!"

"Well, you can help protect them by not telling them how nice some people can be. Then they won't think all people are nice. That way they can't be hurt by the ones who aren't nice. Do you understand?"

Chuga thought about it for a few minutes. "I think so," he said finally.

"I'll tell you what," said Mama, "let's make this our little secret. We can talk about your friend Lilly anytime you want, as long as no one else is around. What do you say?"

"Okay, Mama," he said, knowing she must be right. She was right about everything else, and he didn't want to disappoint her.

For the next few days Chuga wrestled with what Mama said. He decided he didn't want to see his new friends get hurt because of him. He was just so happy to have a friend he was busting to tell someone. He knew if he did tell it would have to be a secret that no one else could tell. But then he would have told himself. *How can you keep someone else from telling a secret, if you can't do it yourself,* he wondered. He decided not to tell, and once satisfied with his decision he started to think about the new friends he'd make. He liked having friends. He liked having someone to play with. Mama said there would be many kids like himself at the Black Pebbled Beach and he couldn't wait to get there.

His excitement could only last so long before impatience set in and he whined at Mama, "Are we there yet?"

"We're almost there, baby," said a weary Mama. She too was tiring of the journey. They had traveled far. They were getting close though. The cooling of the water and arrival of small and large, slow moving icebergs were telltale signs she showed Chuga to lift his spirits.

It was relatively uneventful for the next couple of days when Mama called out to Chuga. "Look, baby. There's a small group of whales heading this way. Maybe they'll let us join them."

And so they did.

9

Soon others joined their growing pod, some in small groups and other lonely stragglers just happy to see them. Their numbers continued to grow as they dodged the growing numbers of icebergs and followed the icy water to its source. Before long they turned a corner around some high reaching cliffs and entered the wide opening into a large, shallow inlet and there it was. The Black Pebbled Beach. Framed by the dark cliffs and rolling dunes of the long valley, and fed by the icy waters of the mountain streams whose white peaks rose high on the horizon, far off in the distance.

Chuga was amazed! He'd never seen anything like it! There were hundreds and hundreds of white whales everywhere his eyes could see. He was overwhelmed by the loud, constant noise of hundreds of conversations and he tucked up under Mama's flippers.

"It's okay, baby," Mama said to comfort him. She remembered the first time she'd arrived at the Black Pebbled Beach and how it scared her too. "You stay right here by my side as we look for Finuga, Kruga and the rest of our friends."

Chuga nodded his consent. This was one time he was for sure going to obey Mama.

They said goodbye to their traveling partners as they collectively branched out in search of their own loved ones. Chuga stayed in constant contact with Mama as they got jostled about by the sheer numbers of white whales while searching for her friend Finuga. He watched from Mama's side as she showed him around and explained why they came here each year. He'd asked her before, when she'd taught him about the ocean currents they followed and the tides that drove the water onto the land, but she wanted to wait till they were here to better explain. She'd shown Chuga the changing temperatures and subtle shifts of the currents that told them when to start their journey. The importance of the timing was because if they arrived too early, there would be no food, and if too late, they'd miss all the many white whales that traveled long and short distances from their homes to be here. And it was a short window - sometimes as little as two weeks, and sometimes as many as four.

He watched as the many white whales swam about chattering away and thrashing about in the shallow waters. There was plenty of room for all of them though many seemed to favor the river's mouth. Mama pointed out the black pebbles of the beach that gave it its name. She showed him the pebbles below them, on the sea floor, and explained how they helped them to shed their old dead skin for the new skin growing underneath. That was why they were thrashing about. They were rubbing their bodies against the pebbles to help with the molting process. She warned Chuga to remember the tides and always be aware of the incoming and outgoing waves. The water was shallow throughout the inlet and just like with Lilly, she'd reminded him, if you weren't careful the tide could carry you away, or leave you stranded on the beach.

Chuga paid close attention, and watched the large waves produced by the incoming tide. He watched them rise as they were funneled into the inlet from the sea beyond, and then rise some more as they reached the stones deposited at the end of the fast moving waters of the rushing river as it entered from the mountains beyond. He watched the waves crash upon the pebbled beach with thundering force as they threw themselves upon the land. He saw the white whales race and thrash about close to the shore. Then much later, he noticed how they backed away from the shore as the tide moved out and left the inlet with calm still water.

As they continued to search for Finuga and friends, Chuga saw many groups – large and small – with kids of all sizes, and adults much bigger than Mama, and he was afraid. He couldn't wait to get here to make some new friends, but now it was too much. There were so many of them, and so much noise! They all seemed to be talking at once, and though he could make out some of the talk, it was too much to follow it all. He remembered Lilly's Daddy calling them the 'canaries of the sea', but he hadn't known what it meant, and forgot to ask Mama later. He thought to ask Mama now, but her attention was elsewhere. He snuggled himself up under her flipper to make sure she didn't forget him, and she gave him a reassuring squeeze. He thought of Lilly and wished he was back with her in the quiet, Pink Sand Beach cove. He missed her so much.

Soon they heard the delighted cries of Finuga as she saw them approach. There was a warm homecoming with hugs and happy greetings from all. They were all very glad to see Jenuga and Chuga and to know they made it safely. Chuga was frightened by it all and stayed safely tucked up under Mama's flipper.

Jenuga greeted her best friend warmly and they each felt the relief flood over them. "And this must be Chuga," said Finuga as she gawked at Chuga, noting his small size. "It doesn't look like he's grown at all. And so shy," she added.

"Yeah," said Mama, "I think he's just frightened by all the excitement. He's never seen so many friends together. Remember your first time here? How scary it was?"

"Yes, of course. Well, let me get Annie over here. She can show him around a little so we can catch up. Annuga!!" she called and they waited for her little girl to arrive.

Jenuga and Finuga chatted about nothing important and soon up swam a small girl who said, "Here I am, Mom."

"There you are," said Finuga.

"Hi, Annie," said Jenuga.

"Hi Jenuga," said Annie. She embraced Jenuga in a firm squeeze of genuine affection and a hint of relief. "I'm so happy you made it. We were worried."

"Thanks Annie," said Jenuga, "it's good to finally be here. And it's good to see you too."

"Annie," said Finuga, "you remember Jenuga's little boy Chuga? I'd like you to help out by playing with him so Jenuga and I can talk."

"Okay," she said and turned to the little white whale. Annie was not very big herself, but she was still almost twice the size of the tiny kid before her. She remembered leaving them behind because he was too small and weak to make the trip when they left weeks ago. This was her second time here at the Black Pebbled Beach so she knew her way around. "Come on," she said and swam a short distance away.

"Stay close," said Jenuga and Finuga in unison, and then Finuga added, "Where we can see you."

"Okay," came Annie's reply, and she waited for the kid to join her.

"Go ahead, baby," said Mama as she gently pushed him away. "You go play with Annie for a while. But not too far," warned Mama again.

Chuga had no desire to be far from Mama's side so he cautiously followed Annie a short distance away. When he was sure it wasn't too far, he looked anxiously at Annie.

"You're awfully small," said Annie as a matter of obvious fact. "How come you're so small?"

"I don't know," Chuga replied defensively.

"It's okay," she said smiling, and added quickly to put him at ease, "I like it! My name is Annuga, but my friends call me Annie," she said, and then paused briefly. When the kid didn't take her cue, she asked, "What's your name again?"

"My name is Chuga," mimicking her introduction, "but my friends call me..." His voice trailed off as he thought about his only friend, Lilly. He remembered what Mama said about their secret and looked at Annie with sad eyes. "Well," he went on, "I guess I don't have any friends yet." And now it was his turn to pause.

"Alright," she said, after pondering for a moment. "You can call me Annie, and I'll be your friend."

Oh boy!, thought Chuga, *my first friend at the Black Pebbled Beach!* He knew he liked Annie right away because of her pretty smile and warm eyes. She didn't seem to mind his small size, and announced their friendship right away. He was very happy, and forgot all about Lilly for a while.

10

Chuga and Annie played together as Jenuga and Finuga huddled together nearby. They had been friends for a long time and would hide nothing from each other. They'd made this journey together many times as both kids, and now parents. Jenuga knew how hard it was for Finuga to leave her and Chuga behind when they weren't ready to travel. She knew Finuga would never have forgiven herself if anything had happened to her and Chuga, but had chased her off just the same. There was a time to go, and they'd waited much too long already. She'd known Finnie must leave and help guide their families to the Black Pebbled Beach. Now that they were reunited, there were many stories to tell. "It's so good to see you Finnie. How was your trip?"

asked Jenny with concern for the friends she'd not yet seen.

"It was hard. We lost two friends along the way," Finnie said in a hushed, sad voice.

"Oh, no!" exclaimed Jenny. "What happened?"

"We can only guess. You know how old Charlie was getting. He just couldn't seem to keep up. We went as slow as we could, but when the Black Beasts appeared we all scattered. Kruga and Donny tried to help Charlie by distracting the Black Beasts, but there wasn't much they could do. When we were able to meet up later only Kruga returned, and he was beat up pretty bad."

"Maybe..." started Jenny, but Finnie cut her off.

"No," she said. "We tried to wait around, but we could hear the joy of the Black Beasts, and had to leave as quickly as we could."

"But..."

"They'd have been here by now," she said, correctly guessing what Jenny was thinking. "We've only been here a few days. After the run-in with the Black Beasts we rushed to get here as fast as we could." They paused in quiet reflection, remembering their lost loved ones.

"How is Annie doing?" Jenny asked. "I know she and Donny were close friends."

"Yeah, it's been difficult for her. He was like a big brother to her. She cried a lot for a few days. But since we arrived here she's met some old friends and made some new ones. She seems to be handling it better. I know she's still sad and really misses him, but she keeps busy. It helps take her mind off it."

"They have to grow up so fast, don't they?" Jenny said. She and Finnie both turned to watch Annie and Chuga playing close by.

"Yeah, it doesn't seem fair sometimes." Finnie said. "But there's only so much you can do."

"Very true. But it helps when you have good friends around to learn and grow with. To share the joy and pain."

"Like us?" Finnie said with a warm smile.

"Yeah, like us," Jenny said with a smile of her own.

"So, how was your trip?" questioned Finnie after a long moment. "Chuga seems so tiny, still."

"He is," said Jenny, "He hasn't seemed to have grown much, but he's strong and he's fast. Quick-fast. He can swim circles around me, and he's very bright, very curious. Always asking questions and exploring or investigating everything. Sometimes to a fault. But he's a good boy - respectful and attentive and mostly mindful."

"Did you have any trouble?" Finnie asked. "I was so worried."

"No, no trouble really. We came close once, but I think we missed most of it because of our tardiness. We did hear and see some Black Beasts a couple weeks ago. Gee, I hope it wasn't Charlie and Donny."

"Oh, I hope not."

"We ducked into the cove with the pink sand beach to hide."

"We stopped there too," said Finnie. "We stopped to rest, hoping you might catch up. When we left, well, that's when the Black Beasts found us. They were waiting for us." They both realized then how close they'd been to finding each other, and the sad truth about the fate of their friends.

"This is just for the two of us," started Jenny after another moment. "I made Chuga promise not to tell anyone, for reasons that will be obvious, and you must not tell anyone either."

"Of course," promised Finnie with piqued interest.

"When we were in the Pink Sand Beach cove," Jenny continued, "we were visited by a small family of people."

"What did you do?"

"We couldn't leave yet, so we hid in the rocks and watched them. Chuga was so fascinated by the little one, he could hardly contain himself. When the little one, Lilly is her name, when she got caught up in the outgoing tide my brave little Chuga dashed out and pushed her to shore! I think he saved her life! Then somehow or another, Chuga and Lilly ended up playing together!"

"What!?!" an exasperated Finnie exclaimed. "How?"

"I'm not sure. But I watched from close by and they had a great time together. They really hit it off. They seemed to understand each other with no problem."

"Incredible," Finnie interrupted, "but how could you let them?"

"I'm not sure that I did," replied Jenny. "I couldn't stop them. I can't remember wanting too either. And neither could her Mommy and Daddy. It only took a few minutes to see it would be okay, and then we couldn't have stopped it if we tried. We all watched from close by, and I could see the joy in her Mommy's face as our eyes met across the way. I knew how she felt, cause I felt it too. There was just no way to deny them!"

"Unbelievable!"

"It didn't last too long before they had to leave, and then later so did we. But for a short while there it was absolutely delightful to watch them have so much fun. When they said their goodbyes you could tell they understood. They hugged and she even kissed him on his little noggin."

"Wow."

"That's not all," continued Jenny, "when we were back on our way, Chuga slowed us a little as he studied the area down to the very last detail. When I asked what he was doing, he told me he wanted to make sure he could find it again. He told me they promised to see each other again someday. And you know, I really hope they do!"

"It's almost unbelievable," said Finnie. "And I can see why you wouldn't want him to tell anyone. Who would believe it?"

"Well, there's that," said Jenny, "and the danger of our friends not being afraid of people. As nice as Lilly and her family are we both know there are many more people who would hurt us. It would be horrible to learn someone was hurt because they didn't think people were dangerous. Especially if they unwittingly tried to play with them knowing our experience and thinking it would be fine."

"Yeah, you're right. I hadn't thought of that. And I can see where others could make that mistake. I guess it makes good sense not to speak of it. But can Chuga keep it to himself?"

"Yes," said Jenny, "I think so. I made sure he understood how important it was. We made it our little secret, so you mustn't say anything to him about it or he might think it's okay to tell his friends because I told mine."

"Don't worry," Finnie said. "Your secret is safe with me. And thanks for telling me. It really is an incredible story."

Jenny and Finnie continued to talk as Annie and Chuga played nearby. They were both so glad to be reunited, and to see their kids playing happily together.

11

For the next few days Chuga stayed close to Mama and Finuga. He was still frightened by the large number of whales in the inlet, and followed them around as they greeted old acquaintances they only saw at these annual gatherings. He played with Annie when she was around, and watched her play with her friends, from afar, when she wasn't. When she asked him to come play with the other kids he fibbed and told her Mama wanted him to stay close by.

One afternoon, while he was still working up his courage, Annie swam straight up to Jenuga and asked if they could go play with the other kids.

"Of course," said Jenuga. "It's about time he made some more friends. Just don't stray too close to the shore. The tide is coming in and you know what that means don't you, baby?"

"Yes, Mama," said Chuga, and he realized he was not going to be able to say no to Annie this time.

"Come on, Chuga," said Annie and she turned and led him away. "I want you to meet some of my friends. They can't wait to meet you."

"Really?" asked Chuga. He forgot his fears and followed Annie into a small group of kids.

"Hey everyone, this is Chuga," said Annie. "Chuga, these are my friends."

One little girl swam close and said "Hi, I'm Sanduga, but everyone calls me Sandy. What was your name again?"

"It's Chuga."

"Chuga," repeated Sandy. "And what do your friends call you?" she asked.

Chuga paused momentarily, confused by the question. He thought of Lilly as he turned to Annie for help. She smiled encouragement but held her tongue. Chuga turned back to Sandy and said, "Uuhh... Chuga?"

"Okay," said Sandy. "I like it! Hi, Chuga, you can call me Sandy."

The rest of the introductions were made and soon he was playing with Annie and her friends Sandy, Susie,

Kara, Bella, Nora, and Mary. It didn't take long before they all commented about his small size, learned what they needed to know, and then quickly forgot about it and invited him into their group. He was the only boy, but no one seemed to take any more notice of that than they did his small size. Soon they were laughing and playing and dashing about. They spent the next few days playing their games and becoming close friends. Chuga was as happy as he could be.

Each night he told Mama about the fun they had, and she was happy about the new friends he was making. She could see he was beginning to relax and enjoy the environment.

The more they played, and the more Chuga learned, the more curious he became. He'd noticed a large group of bigger kids playing closer to shore and asked Annie about them. They were playing some kind of interesting game that puzzled Chuga. It was like the game of tag he played with his new friends, but they seemed to not be chasing each other as he and his friends were.

"Who are they?" Chuga asked. "And what kind of game are they playing?" pointing in their direction.

"They're the older kids," replied Annie. "And they're trying to ride the waves."

"How do you do that?"

"I'm not sure. I guess it's fun if you catch one right, but I've never tried it. It seems like a lot of work for such a short ride." They watched as each took a turn, waiting for the next wave to come, then kicking hard trying to push themselves up the front of the wave as it passed. The wave would lift them for a second then curl over them as it raced to the shore, and they ducked under before the inevitable crash. Some were carried along in front of the swells while others were immediately gobbled up by its force and pulled back under. It looked like fun. "Besides, they don't want to play with us. They think we're too young."

"Who's that big one in the middle?" Chuga asked, staring in wonder at the biggest kid he'd ever seen.

"That's Barruga," said Annie in a not so friendly tone. He's my cousin. Stay as far away from him as you can," she continued. "He's a bully."

The rest of their group had gathered around and now nodded their agreement.

"What's a bully?" asked Chuga.

"It's someone who makes you do things when you don't want to," chimed in Bella.

"Yeah, and he picks on us all the time," added Kara.

"That's right!" said Nora, not wanting to be left out. "He's big and mean and always telling you what to do."

"Just stick with us and we'll keep him away from you as best we can," said Annie. She knew what kind of trouble Barruga could cause. She was hoping they could avoid him because there was no telling what he'd do if he met Chuga. She knew Chuga would never stand a chance with Barruga. He was three times Chuga's size and as big as Chuga was small. She turned away, putting her large cousin out of her mind, rejoining the game they'd started.

Chuga hesitated for a moment, still fascinated by the unfamiliar game, and awed by Barruga's sheer size. He was rightfully afraid of Barruga because of his friends warnings, but unable to put the bully and the wave riding out of his mind.

Over the next few days, Chuga and his new friends began to attract the attention of some of the other kids in the inlet. Just as Chuga was struck by Barruga's large size, some of the others were equally interested in his small size. Some of the smaller ones began sneaking away from Barruga's crowd and soon more and more kids drifted in to join their play. They all seemed to know Annie, and she introduced them to Chuga and the other girls as they filtered in. They all wanted to know why Chuga was so small, and before he could answer Annie would say 'he just is,' and that would be the end of it. They accepted her explanation and just as quickly accepted Chuga on her word.

"How do you remember all their names?" Chuga asked one night as he was struggling with this new problem.

"Oh, don't worry," came her reply. "You'll remember them the more you play with them. The hard part is remembering them next year when you haven't seen them for a while!"

This did not make Chuga feel any better about his problem, and reminded him that they would soon have to leave these waters, and his new friends, to head south. He was happy that Annie and Finuga were coming with Mama and him, along with Bella and Susie and their families. It also reminded him of Lilly, and he wondered if he would see her again soon. He wanted Annie to meet her, even though he hadn't told her about Lilly. He thought if they went back to the Pink Sand Beach cove and Lilly was there, it would have to be okay with Mama.

There was so much to think about in this world.

12

The White Beast continued his journey towards the sea, scavenging the land for food to appease his aching belly. He followed the rushing river as it grew with the addition of the melting snow. He stopped now and then to gobble up the semi-frozen fish he found washed up on the swollen banks, or to dig in the damp black sand for the small clams that hid from the warming sun. He would sniff the air from time to time, hoping for a sign. Days passed and his hunger grew. The few fish and plentiful clams helped, but what he ached for was the blubber of a fatted seal or the like. So he lumbered on, trying to ignore his growing hunger.

13

Barruga began to notice there were less and less kids in his group. For the last couple of days it seemed more and more were sneaking away without his permission. At first it made him mad, then he saw they were mostly the smallest and weakest, and he let it slide. He soon realized his mistake. If he let one go, they would all eventually leave, and he would lose his hold over them. It was time to put an end to this once and for all. He abandoned the wave he was unsuccessfully trying to catch, and inquired of his remaining group about the missing kids. Getting only blank stares in return, he searched the surrounding waters for the deserters. He found some gathered together on the far side of the inlet with that little Miss Goody-Twofins cousin of his, Annuga. He liked Annie. They used to be friends. They used to play together before he got so big. Before he stopped playing with her because she was a girl. And before he learned he could use his size to his advantage. He allowed her to have her little group of girlfriends because they were of no use to him anyway. But she was still dangerous. She was the only one who stood up to him, and it set a bad example for all the rest. He couldn't let her get away with it or he might end up lonely again. And that was the last thing he wanted. So he gathered up his remaining group with a stern command, and they raced over to investigate.

14

Annie, Chuga, and their group were playing twenty questions. It was Chuga's turn because he guessed right about Susie being a starfish. He was excited. He thought he had a good one that nobody would get right.

"Okay, what am I?" He asked the small group.

Annie asked the first question. "Do you live on land?"

"No," came his reply.

Bella was next, "Do you live in the sea?"

"Yes."

Susie: "Do you have legs and walk on the bottom?"

"No."

Kara: "Do you swim through the water?"

"Yes."

Mary: "Are you some kind of fish?"

"Yes."

Annie: "Wait, that's not fair. There are thousands of different kinds of fish."

Chuga: "Yes, but I'm special."

Annie: "Then are you a..."

Nora: "Wait!" She cut Annie off. "It's not your turn."

Annie: "Okay. But I think I know what you are," she said with a knowing smile at Chuga. He smiled back and now she was sure.

Nora: "That's not fair." She'd caught their little exchange.

Annie: "It's okay, I won't guess again. Go ahead, it's your turn."

Nora paused and thought for a moment, trying to figure out what Annie might know. "Are you a colorful fish?"

"No."

Sara: "Are you bigger than me?"

"No."

Sandy: "Are you a bottom feeding fish who digs a home in the sand and sneaks out to eat and play?"

"No."

Manny (one of two small boys who'd joined their growing group): "Do you carry your home with you?"

"No."

Jake (the other): "How could he be, you dummy. He said he was a special kind of fish. Not a crab or a snail or a turtle, right?"

Chuga: "Is that a question?"

Jake: "No!" he said quickly, not wanting to waste his question, or seem like a dummy too.

Annie: "Okay, then ask your question, but no more name calling. We don't do that here."

Jake: "I'm sorry, Manny. I didn't mean it. Can he have another question?" he asked the group and Chuga in particular.

Manny: "It's okay, Jake. It was my mistake. Go ahead."

Jake: "Are you a scary fish with big teeth?"

"No."

Annie: "That's ten, half way there. Your turn again Bella."

Bella: "Are you a Jellyfish?" she asked, thinking she figured it out, but disappointed when Chuga answered.

"No."

Susie: "Do you have flippers and a tailfin?"

"Yes."

Kara: "Are you a Sailfish?"

"No."

Mary: "Are you a tiny fish that swims in great bunches?"

"No."

Nora: "So you're not too big, and not too small, but do you still swim with a school of others?"

"Yes."

Sara: "Can I eat you?"

"Yes, if you can catch me." Chuga replied with a giggle.

Sandy: "Are you a salmon?"

"No."

Manny: "Are you a codfish?"

"No."

Jake: "Are you a halibut?"

"No"

Annie: "Okay, last question." She was still excited because she knew what he was, and the rest of them were stumped. "It's your turn again Bella."

Bella: "Okay, Annie. We give up. What kind of fish is he?"

All the kids nodded to Annie. She looked at Chuga and he had a big smile on his face. He couldn't wait for them to find out, so he nodded his consent to her also. "He's a flying fish, right?" she asked Chuga.

"Yes, I am!" replied Chuga with genuine delight.

"What's a flying fish?" asked Manny. He'd never seen or heard of such a thing.

"It's a fish that swims but can also fly!" Chuga said with great respect. He described the ones he'd seen, and they all listened with rapt attention but great disbelief.

"Wow," said Jake.

"No way," said Nora. "You're making that up. He's making that up, right Annie?"

"Yeah, he's pulling our tailfins, right Annie?" added Bella.

"No," said Annie. "I thought so too when he told me about them, but I asked his mother and she said it was true. She said she wouldn't have believed it herself if she hadn't seen it with her own eyes."

"Wow," said Jake again. They all knew Annie wouldn't lie.

They all looked at Chuga with great admiration, and he beamed with pride.

15

"Okay," said Annie, "who's next?" There was a long pause while everyone tried to think of something to top Chuga's flying fish, but failed.

"It's your turn Annie, you guessed right." Kara said.

"Alright," declared Annie, "I'll go. Who am....," she started to ask when suddenly Barruga bullied his way to the middle of the small group.

"What's going on here!" he bellowed in a deep, low voice. He towered over the small kids and growled his displeasure.

Annie quickly positioned herself between Chuga and Barruga as the other kids were muscled to the outside by the bigger kids. She said, "Nothing's going on here! We're playing. So why don't you go away and leave us alone." She stood her ground, but Barruga wasn't backing down, and it frightened her.

Barruga knew not to mess with Annie, but his pride was at stake. He sensed her protective stance and tried to see what she was hiding. "What is it," he ordered, waiting for her to comply. He moved one way then the other trying to see behind her as the other kids shrank away in fear. "What are you hiding?"

Annie mirrored his movements, trying desperately to hide Chuga from him. She and Barruga locked eyes. They stared each other down for a long moment as the fate of the group hung in the balance. None of the other kids dared make a sound as the tension grew!

Annie knew what would happen if she couldn't make Barruga back down. She had to protect Chuga.

Barruga knew his authority was being tested by Annie, but he'd come this far and was not stopping now. There was too much at stake.

Barruga finally advanced on Annie and shoved her aside, leaving him face to face with Chuga. "What's this little runt?" Barruga asked, momentarily thrown off by the little whale who was near a third his size. He'd never seen one so small and for a split second thought he might make a good meal.

Annie shot up next to Chuga. "This is my friend, Chuga," she said, "You leave him alone!" She tried to stare him down again, but Barruga was already too mad and too confused by the little kid.

"Chuga? What kinda name is that? Huh, little Chewy," taunted Barruga as he remembered his first thought about a meal. He chuckled at his own play on words.

Annie pushed her way in front of Chuga and once again faced off with Barruga. "Don't call him that!" She barked. "His name is Chuga!"

"Why, he's just a little pipsqueak," laughed Barruga, and stared right back at Annie and the other kids, just daring them to disagree.

The other kids were too scared to speak or run, and shrank back even more from the confrontation.

"Leave him alone," shouted Annie. "We were playing. Why don't you just go away and leave us alone?"

"Well, maybe he wants to play with me," retorted Barruga. "Whaddya say pipsqueak, wanna come play with me?"

Chuga was still new to this friend thing, but he didn't think he liked being called a pipsqueak. Barruga was huge, and he figured the name must have something to do with his own small size. When he saw the others cringe at its use he was sure it wasn't a good thing.

He was very happy to see his friend Annie stand up for him, but he remembered watching them play and was still very curious. "What are you playing?" he asked innocently, hoping to learn more about the games he'd seen them play.

"We're riding waves," said Barruga though everyone who'd seen him try knew he was unable to catch one. "Come on over and try it. There's some really good ones coming in right now."

Chuga glanced over at the incoming waves and again was curious, but looked back at Barruga and said earnestly, "I can't right now. The tide is going out, and Mama said to stay away from the shore. It's dangerous."

"What's all this mumbo jumbo about," bellowed Barruga.

Annie and the rest of the kids knew right away that Chuga had said the wrong thing. "Stop it!" yelled Annie in Barruga's face, and there were murmurs of consent through the ranks.

Barruga could feel he was losing his edge, so he pressed on. "Did you just say your mommy said not to, pipsqueak?" His face lit up as the light went on in his head. "Are you a mama's boy? Poor wittle mama's boy can't come out and pway. It's too dangewous," he taunted.

Chuga didn't like being called a pipsqueak even if he didn't know what it meant. But he knew what a mama's boy was and it wasn't a good thing except when Mama said it. He didn't know how to respond, and was afraid of what he might say, so he kept quiet as Barruga carried on.

"Are you a..." started Barruga. He paused for full effect. "Dare I say it... Could it be?..." and now he had everyone's full attention.

They let out a collective groan because they knew what was coming. They'd all heard it before, many being the focus of this same childish rant. Only Chuga was unaware of what was to come, and everyone else understood there was no stopping it. He didn't have a chance, and he wouldn't have to wait long.

"Are you a scaredy-fish?" Barruga finished with a triumphant grin.

"Oh no," said Annie under her breath as the group gasped in horror. "Stop it Barruga, you bully!" she pleaded. "Leave him alone, he's just a little kid!" She tried to lead Chuga away but was blocked by Barruga. He was in his element now! He had them all right where he wanted them and wasn't about to let up. It was time to punish all of them for ignoring him!

"I asked you a question, pipsqueak! Are you a scaredy-fish?"

Chuga didn't know what a scaredy-fish was either, but he could tell by the reaction of the group it was bad. Really bad. Now he was scared, and he could feel the tears welling up in his eyes. He wanted Mama. He knew he couldn't cry or it would somehow make it worse, and maybe that's what a scaredy-fish was in the first place.

"But Mama said..." he began before even he realized it was the wrong thing to say.

Barruga beamed with delight. There was fire in his eyes and he started chanting. "Scaredy-fish, scaredy-fish, Chuga is a scaredy-fish," over and over. He began swimming tight circles around Chuga and Annie, staring the other kids in the group down as he passed. He would not let up, chanting and chanting, daring the others not to join in with his menacing stare.

Slowly and softly, the others began to join in. They too were scared beyond control. They did not want to embolden Barruga, but it was the only way to escape his wrath, both now and later, when he got them alone. And he would get them alone. He would remember, and he would get his revenge.

Soon all the new kids were chanting loudly and Annie started to cry. Bella and the rest of the younger kids hid their faces behind the bigger kids, and held their tongues. They were too afraid of Barruga to leave, but couldn't bear to join in, no matter what. Some started to weep softly and were drowned out by the growing chant.

Chuga wanted to get away but the chanting mob was closing in on he and Annie and Barruga. Closer and closer, louder and louder!

Jenuga and Finuga heard the commotion along with the rest of the pod. They started to watch more closely, and drift towards the growing group.

Bella raced to them and barely got out Chuga's name before Jenuga took off toward the chanting, frenzied mob! As she reached the outside of the uncontrolled mob she heard her baby's desperate cry of anguish. "Chuga, no!" she cried in despair, but it was too late. He was already moving.

"Scaredy-fish, scaredy-fish, Chuga is a scaredy-fish!" continued the mob, pushing closer and closer, unable to stop themselves. Chuga was about to burst into tears. He didn't know what he did to deserve this, and he didn't know what to do - how to make it stop. "I'm not a scaredy-fish!" he cried.

"Stop it!" yelled Annie in vain.

Barruga was thrilled as he continued to lead the chant.

"Scaredy-fish, scaredy-fish, Chuga is a scaredy-fish!" cried the mob. They pushed in around Chuga as he frantically searched for a way out.

Chuga heard Mama's cry and it triggered a reaction from her many lessons. He dove down under the swelling, morphing mob, just sneaking through where only he and his small frame could go. He was forced down by the throbbing mass, scraping his soft belly along the pebbles of the bottom, and broke free before they realized he was gone. He wanted to go to Mama and let her protect him. But she was back there, working her way to the middle of the throng, yelling for them to stop! He knew he couldn't go back to face the mob or he would always be known as the little pipsqueak, and the mama's boy. The scaredy-fish! He couldn't run away because it wouldn't solve anything either. He didn't know where to go.

He could go to the Pink Sand Beach and find Lilly, but what if she wasn't there. Then he'd be all alone, and that thought scared him even more.

There was only one thing he could think of, and it was right in front of him! If he wanted to show he wasn't any of the things Barruga was calling him, then he must prove him wrong!

Chuga set his sights squarely on the rolling swells of the incoming waves and dashed off in their direction. He looked for the smallest one he could find and settled on the last one in the set. He was too late to get in front of it as he'd seen the others do, so he slid in behind it. With a powerful flick of his tailfin he chased up the back of the wave as it began to crest. He pushed to the top of the swell as it continued to grow, building and building into an enormous mound of rolling water. It pulled at him as it climbed, trying to suck him under as it reached for the sky! He saw the curl begin to form as he watched the waves ahead crash one by one onto the beach, and then pull back to the sea, further driving his wave upward. He struggled with all his might to reach the top and not get dragged under. It roared like thunder as the curl reached over like a closing fist and hurtled itself at the approaching shoreline.

Behind him, Jenuga, Annie, Barruga and the others were just realizing he was gone. Looking about frantically, they searched for him as the chanting slowly lost its steam. Confused and newly ashamed, the kids collided with each other in the confusion, trying to be the first to spot him.

Suddenly, a cry rang out from Bella, who was still at Finuga's side, watching from a distance. The whole pod – drawn by the loud chanting of the frenzied mob, and now all completely caught up in the unfolding drama – jerked their heads around to the sound of Bella's alarm. She pointed with her flipper and all eyes followed her stare as they turned in time to see Chuga suddenly break free of the wave's strong grip, and shoot to the top of the wave. They watched in stunned silence as the monster wave carried Chuga on its back and raced along.

Chuga was about to abandon the growing wave when he felt it lift him up, and loosen its grip on him. Instantly he felt free and totally alive! His body felt weightless as the water churned beneath him. He was flying! *So this is what it felt like to fly* he thought, as he spread his flippers wide and sailed along on the wind, held high by the crest of the wave. He closed his eyes and felt the wind whip his face, forgetting everything around him. He rode the wave as if he owned it, and though it only lasted a few glorious moments, he felt like it lasted forever. He lost himself in the feeling. He thought of the birds and the flying fish and knew what they knew. *Oh, what a feeling,* he thought with utter joy!

The rest of the pod saw him stretch out his flippers, and gasped as they watched him soar by. The stunned silence was broken by those who found their voice enough to shout what everyone else knew. "He's flying," they cheered and cries of joy and wonder rolled through the masses. Chuga was indeed flying!

It only lasted a few prolonged moments before the wave reached its end along the pebbled beach. There were only three whales who turned away in the end.

Barruga turned away in disgust. He had pushed the kid to the brink, and now he was quickly becoming a legend right before his eyes. He knew no one would ever forget this day, and his unsavory part in it. They had won. No one would follow his orders now. He would be alone again with no friends. No one to play with, or more accurately, no one to boss around anymore. When he looked back there was hate in his eyes.

Jenuga couldn't watch because she saw what no one else saw.

Annie looked away because she felt the fear ripple through Jenuga's side, and searched the horizon for its source. Soon everyone would know the cause of Jenuga's fear, and it would change the day's mood and direction for a third and final dramatic time. When they looked back, it was already too late.

But this was a day that would not soon be forgotten. Yes, *this* day! The day a small white whale named Chuga flew like a bird across the sky! The day a legend was born!

16

The white whales cheered with un-restrained glee and admiration as the mighty wave crashed in a spectacular display of flying water and white foam, while carrying Chuga onto the beach and gently placing him high upon the pebbled shore. As its remains raced back to the sea it spun Chuga back to face his adoring crowd.

Chuga was ecstatic! His heart raced and his eyes shown bright as he bowed to his amazed audience. He lifted his head high and yelled, "That was great!" And all the kids cheered. All except Barruga.

Chuga had flown like a bird, and everyone had witnessed it. He was a hero! Not a scaredy-fish, or a pipsqueak, or a mama's boy, but a real life hero! His smile reached from eye to eye as he let the cheers roll over him. His eyes swept across the inlet and he basked in the glory as the cheers continued to rain down and roll sweetly over him. He searched for his friends and found Barruga's eyes and saw only hatred. When he found Mama and Annie together, he did not see joy, but fear, and could not understand why.

But that was all that was rolling over him. When the next waves hit the beach they came up woefully short of reaching him. The next wave showed promise, but fell short again, weakly pushing its mass several feet short of Chuga's perch.

He suddenly realized what Mama had foreseen already, and now he understood. The tide had turned. There would be no more waves forthcoming.

With each successive wave showing less and less interest in his plight, it became apparent he was not joining them in the celebration. The pod soon realized this new danger and the cheers dwindled swiftly to stunned silence. This couldn't be happening! One moment there was joy and jubilation, and now only fear and disbelief! An impending doom swept through them with breakneck speed as they finally saw what Jenuga already knew.

"Mama," cried Chuga in a scared, pleading voice. The full weight of his predicament engulfed him.

"I'm here, baby," said Mama, trying to hide the fear from her voice. She swam as close as she dared to where he lay stranded.

"I'm sorry, Mama," Chuga offered in defeat.

"You must fight, baby. You can't give up. When the next wave comes you must fight with all your might to try to reach the water."

"Okay, Mama," Chuga replied as the next wave gently splashed far in front of him. He kicked and squirmed and wiggled his little body, but was unable to move forward. Instead, he only managed to dig himself deeper into the pebbles, creating a nest under himself. "It's not coming close enough," he told Mama when he stopped struggling.

"Okay, baby," said Mama in a soft soothing tone. "Now you listen to me good, okay?"

"Yes, Mama."

"We talked about the tides before, do you remember?"

"Yes Mama, I'm so sorry," he apologized again softly, thinking she was mad at him.

"It's okay, baby. You have to hang in there now. The tide will come back like it always does. So, you must be strong till it does. You remember about the tides, don't you?"

"Yes, Mama," said Chuga with a faint glimmer of hope in his voice. "I'll be strong."

"Good boy. I'm right here and I'm not going any-
where. We'll get through this together, but it's going to
take a while for the tide to return so you need to stay
calm. I'm not going to lie to you, this is as bad as it gets,
and it may get worse before it gets better. You just have
to hang in there and we'll make it somehow. I know it's
hard, but that's why you must be strong. Understand?"

"Yes, Mama."

"Okay, baby, you rest now and save your energy.
When the tide does return we will have to be ready. You
will need to fight hard to come back to me."

Terrified, he said, "Yes, Mama." and laid his head
down on the pebbled beach to wait. Mama wouldn't lie
to him, and she told him like it was. He didn't know
what might happen, but he knew he would fight for her.

Annie listened to Jenuga's words of encouragement to Chuga and was amazed at how calm and sup-
portive she was being. Her stomach was churning in
fright and she could hardly breathe. She wanted to be
there for her friend but couldn't stop thinking of all
the bad things that could happen. She wished Donny
was here. None of this would have happened if he was.
He would have stopped Barruga. He'd told her once,

'You do what's right, and don't worry about what's left.' Donny was gone because he chose to do the right thing. He tried to save his father. He'd been big and strong, but not a bully like Barruga. He was gentle and kind. He'd been her best friend. Annie couldn't bear the thought of losing another friend so soon. It was too much for her to think about so she swam to her mother's side and wept softly.

Finuga hung back from the beach and kept watch over the whole area. She held Annie close and tried to comfort her. She could feel the anguish and despair in her young girl. Her heart went out to her friend Jennie. But she had a job to do. So she continuously scanned the horizon, wary of the dangers that loomed beyond her sight, ready to call out the alarm if necessary. She hoped she wouldn't have to.

Annie's friends gathered around her for support. They wept quietly at a safe distance where Chuga could not hear. They hushed the youngest kids who had no real understanding of the dangers, and still wanted to play. From time to time they took turns at Jenuga's side showering Chuga with soft words of comfort and support.

Kruga and the older whales patrolled the shallow waters trying to keep busy. Some of the older kids caught some fish and tried to fling them onto the beach where Chuga could reach. It didn't work, and most of the fish accomplished what Chuga could not, and flopped their way back into the water, only to be gobbled up by hungry mouths.

The rest of the white whales milled silently about while they listened to Jenuga and Chuga. They knew it was going to be a long wait. With sprinkled calls of subdued encouragement they watched the time go by, unable to find the energy or desire to do much else. Mothers soothed the fears of their kids and held them close, feeling the premature sting of pain and loss.

Barruga's sudden hate for Chuga gave him a moment of total joy! He couldn't believe the little scaredy-fish had turned the tables on him. First he escaped the delicious taunting, then, instead of running to his poor mommy's side crying like a baby, he'd chased into the waves. For all his trying, Barruga had never been able to ride a wave properly, and it galled him that Chuga had not only ridden one, but a monster! He had watched as the kid hung high in the air, flying past in front of everyone! They were all cheering wildly for him, and Barruga was forgotten. He knew he'd lost his hold over them. They had a hero! When Chuga landed on the beach, turned and shouted, Barruga knew his fate was sealed. He wanted to kill the little pipsqueak, and soon realized along with the rest that he would not get that chance. He knew death would come for Chuga as he lay stranded on the beach. No whale could survive for long outside of the water.

Barruga's joy was not long lived. He realized before anyone else that he would be blamed for what was happening. His days were numbered just like Chuga's days seemed to be. There was no turning back, and no way to repair the damage he'd done. A moment's selfish actions had ruined his life forever. His shame turned his hatred and joy into sadness and fear. Before anyone noticed, he slipped away to the mouth of the inlet, hovering there momentarily, pondering his fate.

17

The White Beast stopped in his tracks when he saw the smaller polar bear with its two cubs in the distance. He stared at her as she caught his movements. His stomach rumbled as he gazed longingly at the cubs, and his mouth watered. This was his territory, and they were intruders. Her cubs would make a healthy meal, and it was her fault for venturing into his homeland. He took up the chase. They had a good lead and didn't hesitate when he made his move. He raced after them for a short while without gaining much ground. He was weak, and could not get the energy to chase them down. He eventually gave up and watched them disappear over the horizon, hanging his head in defeat. He laid on the cold ground to rest, his empty stomach aching with hunger. Soon he would have to return to the raging river that led to the sea. There was food there, and he needed it badly.

18

Barruga's anger and hate for Chuga continued to drain from his body as he looked back from the mouth of the inlet. This was not what he wanted. He just wanted some friends. He wanted someone to play with. He knew he would be blamed for egging Chuga on with his taunts, thus causing this horrible crisis. Feeling like a coward, he slinked out of the inlet and slowly swam away.

Barruga knew he was a bully. He didn't want to be a bully. He told himself it wasn't his fault, but he knew that wasn't true. He was bigger by far than the other kids his age. That was true, but he was the one who made the choice to use his size to his advantage. He didn't at first, but he was too big and clumsy, and no one seemed to like him or want to play with him. Except for Annie, but she was a girl! And she was always hanging around with that big lug, Donny. At least until he didn't show up this year.

The older kids said he was too young, and the kids his age said he was too big and slow. He soon learned they were afraid of him because of his size, and would do what he said if he threatened to pound them. He could make them play with him even if they didn't like him. He knew they tried to avoid him, as even Annie did now. She once said he'd have lots of friends if he wasn't such a bully. He'd pretended not to hear her then, but often wondered if she was right. He had become a bully so the others wouldn't make fun of him and so he could make them play with him. He wished he could be like the rest of them. *Why did he have to be so big?*

He knew he was to blame. The others were sure to hate him. That was nothing new. He knew now that he would no longer be welcome in the pod. It seemed that everyone loved Chuga. He felt terrible for the danger he'd put him in. He'd never really hurt anyone before. But as he thought about Chuga, helplessly stranded on the beach, he knew that had changed forever.

He was convinced he would not get a chance to change now, after the trouble he caused. His only hope, he thought, was to find another pod somewhere and hope they never heard of either himself or Chuga. Good luck with that. After watching Chuga himself, he knew every creature in the sea would soon hear about the white whale who flew like a bird! They'd know. They'd know about him too, and he would not be welcome. He promised himself if he ever got another chance there would be no more bullying for him.

As he drifted aimlessly away, he heard the faint sounds of chanting coming from the inlet he'd abandoned. It made him pause. Could it be? Was Chuga rescued? Was he safe? He strained to hear, but it was not a sound of joy.

It did make him realize, no matter what happened, he needed to know how things would turn out for Chuga. He needed to know if Chuga was going to be safe, or not. If so, he could leave happy. If not, it would be a fitting penance for him to see the end.

So he turned back to the Black Pebbled Beach. When he reached the high cliffs that marked the entrance to the inlet, he realized what the chants were saying. His heart sank. Afraid for his life, he almost fled again. Instead, he squeezed his large frame into the cracks in the rocks and ice, and found a place where he could see the inlet, and not be seen if he kept his head down, and stayed quiet.

19

Inside the inlet, the pod was getting crabby. There was not much they could do to help, and their emotions swung from despair to anger. The older kids were feeling guilty for their part in what happened, and started whispering amongst themselves. Their frustration was mounting. They needed something to lash out at, someone to blame. They picked Barruga. 'It was all his fault,' they reasoned, and soon began the search. They wanted to beat him up or chase him away for what he did. For what he made them do. The whispers grew louder and the group gathered strength.

Luckily for Barruga, he was far from the inlet when they searched among the rocks and ice where he would eventually find his vantage point. When they could not find Barruga, and figured he'd run away, their frustration hit its peak! Soon the angry chant that Barruga heard from afar began to take its voice. First one, then another, then even more joined in. It swiftly escalated into a thunderous shout!

"Scaredy-fish, scaredy-fish, Barruga is a scaredy-fish!" They chanted over and over, gaining in volume with each new voice that joined in. "Scaredy-fish, scaredy-fish, Barruga is a scaredy-fish!"

It continued until they heard Jenuga shriek at the top of her lungs, "Stop it! Stop it right now! This is not helping anyone! It's what started this whole mess in the first place! Blaming Barruga or anyone else is not the answer! It's not going to resolve anything!" She lowered her voice as the sudden anger drained from her. "If you can't say anything encouraging to my Chuga, then please don't say anything at all." She turned her attention back to her baby as the inlet went dead silent around her.

The kids hung their heads in shame and scurried once again to the sides of their beckoning mothers.

Annie was again impressed by Jenuga's courage and strength in the face of the great danger to her baby. She promised herself she would cry no more. She would be strong.

Chuga listened to the chants, and then Mama's pleas. He could hear the panic in her voice. He wanted to be in her flippers, to comfort her. He knew he let her down. He'd told himself over and over he wouldn't, yet here he was stranded on the beach with no one to blame but himself. He had no hatred for Barruga. He'd allowed himself to be swayed by the same chanting mob, and his own desire to fit in. He made a bad choice. Then he'd been swept away by the power of the wave and the joy of the ride. He'd been so happy to be the focus of all the cheers and adulation that he'd failed to recognize the danger till it was too late. Now he was stuck. And Mama was sad and frightened. He vowed again to himself not to give up.

Barruga heard all this while sneaking into his hiding place among the rocks and ice. *I am a scaredy-fish,* he thought and sunk into despair. He was too scared to be alone, and too scared to face his accusers and beg for their forgiveness. He struggled with his thoughts. He decided to stay hidden and watch what happened, or run if anyone stumbled upon him. So, he watched and waited all through the long hours along with the rest of the white whales.

20

The land of the midnight sun was not kind to Chuga on this day. The day had started windy and overcast, and the choppy surf helped to give the waves their strength. Now, as Chuga lay helpless on the pebbled beach, the wind conspired to push the clouds further north, and exposed the sun. Time passed slowly. Seconds felt like minutes, minutes like hours, and the hours seemed to stretch to the length of days.

The sun, now free of the clouds, beat down relentlessly upon Chuga as it crept its way across the sky. It gathered up heat from the black pebbles and baked Chuga's defenseless body. Chuga's skin began to crack with the lack of moisture it needed to thrive. Short knife-like wounds began to show and continued to grow slowly but steadily across his exposed back. He was growing weaker by the hour.

He thought about Mama, and Annie, and his new friends. He thought about Lilly, who he promised to see again. He knew he must be strong like Mama said. His small size and light weight now worked to his advantage. Any larger and his own weight would eventually collapse his lungs and he would suffocate. His thoughts raced wildly from rescue to death and everything in between. He tried to concentrate only on Mama's soft encouraging voice, and knew he could never give up. The tide would come.

The time slowly and methodically marched on, unhurried by the hopes of the anxious onlookers. Unease ruled the day.

21

The White Beast raked the damp, black sand and drew the small clam from its shallow perch. With his large claws, and with practiced ease, he quickly cracked open the tiny morsel and greedily sucked up its prize. He licked the shell clean then lifted his head high to stretch his sore neck. He sniffed the air then searched around the hole-filled beach, intent on finding a fresh spot to dig. As he lowered his head to the present task, he hesitated as a thought invaded his mind. He snapped his sensitive snout back to the air and sniffed again. *Yes, there it is,* he thought as the unmistakable scent barely caressed his nose. He lurched up onto his hind legs and pirouetted slowly, trying to pinpoint the direction of the delicious scent. It was there alright, coming from the sea, carried by the strong breeze that swept across the white, snowy plains of the valley, and ruffled the fur that sagged from his hungry belly. The smell of death. The smell of rotting flesh. The smell of his next meal softly riding the wind, beckoning him. The White Beast crashed to the ground with a mighty thud, licked his lips greedily, snorted loudly, and took his first few steps in the direction of the wind. Forgetting the unfinished task at hand, he gathered speed till he reached a comfortable trot and settled into it. His stomach rumbled in anticipation and drove him on in his dogged pursuit.

22

The light dimmed as the sun rolled low in the sky and hung along the curve of the land on the distant horizon. The dusk settled in for its brief but welcomed visit as one day eased into the next. The moon glistened on the opposite horizon as it made a brief visit to the night sky. The cool air slowed the spread of Chuga's festering wounds, and brought some relief. The new day held the promise of a new tide, and rescue.

With agonizingly slow speed the land began to brighten as the sun once again climbed into the blue skies above. The inlet was calm and quiet as nervous anticipation and faint hope greeted the light.

The sun's warmth soon worked its charms and the cuts on Chuga's back grew slowly giving off the unmistakable odor of rotting flesh.

The seabirds found the scent and followed it to its source. They began to arrive in large numbers, circled above as they located their quarry, and settled in for the coming feast.

Chuga recognized the gathering flock for the hungry mob it was. He knew they dared not attack him while he was alive, but they had sensed his peril, and were gathering in steadily increasing numbers awaiting his untimely demise, and the feast it would provide.

Jenuga knew the arrival of the seabirds meant the smell of death was in the air, and it would attract even more scavengers. There was only one thing that could save her baby, and it was still far from its return.

The seabirds caught the attention of the Black Beasts and soon they were patrolling the waters near the mouth of the inlet. They were unable to safely enter the shallow waters of the large inlet during low tide, which was one of the main reasons it was so popular with the white whales. Even during the high tides, the whales would huddle in the shallows just out of the reach of the Black Beasts. Most times the Black Beasts knew this and avoided the inlet, favoring the deeper waters beyond, and waiting for the white whales to leave. Today there was the smell of flesh in the air and they came close to investigate. They saw the tiny beached whale and lost interest. They took a curious interest in Barruga as he hid in the rocks and ice, but he was also out of their reach, and they soon moved on to more promising ventures.

23

The White Beast ambled along through the short hour of dusk, and never saw the moon at his back. As the sun gradually climbed back into the morning sky it was greeted with the promise of a beautiful day. When the White Beast crested the next dune the smell carried by the distant ocean breeze had grown stronger. He filled his snout with the smell of fresh meat, of warm blood, and of fear. He could see the seabirds gathering on the distant horizon, framed against the deep blue sky. He knew he was getting close and he picked up his pace. His empty stomach rumbled its discomfort and drove him on.

24

As the day took hold, the tension mounted with each passing minute. The pod milled about listlessly as they waited for signs of the returning tide.

The seabirds grew restless as they stalked the pebbled beach around Chuga, shrieking their displeasure.

Jenuga and Annie – who refused to leave Jenuga's side – clung to their fading hopes as Chuga began to show fewer signs of life.

Barruga felt his helplessness turning to anger as he tried to will the uncaring tide to return.

For the next couple of hours they measured the time. In the dead, calm waters of the inlet nary a ripple showed. They were all on their last frayed nerves.

It was Barruga who felt it first from his hiding spot among the rocks and ice. Just a slight shift in the energy of the sea, but it was enough. The tide had arrived! His anger melted away and he danced silently with joy. Chuga was saved! He wanted to rush into the inlet with the good news, but held back, still fearful of the reaction it might cause. He hesitated.

Finuga felt it next. She nearly burst with relief, and frightened poor Bella and Susie, who had taken up the vigil by her side.

Then Jenuga felt it too. Her relief was overwhelming. She could feel the beginning tendrils of hope surge through her. She called out to Chuga in a soft voice to 'hang on.' She didn't want to get his hopes up too high, too fast. The tide was back, but it would still take a while before it made any significant progress. There was still a chance it may not reach him even at its full height. She didn't want to think about that, so she forced the thought into the back of her head and refused to acknowledge it again.

Soon others were aware of it too, and they watched the tide push small ripples against the warm dry pebbles on the shore. There was a new feeling sweeping through the pod. The energy level rose quickly and spurred the seabirds into flight. Whispered murmurs of hope began to spread.

For the next hour they were increasingly hopeful. They watched the waves roll in, gently at first, and then slowly gaining speed and strength as they came. When the first significant wave arrived it was welcomed by triumphant cheers across the inlet. It stretched its reach within a few tantalizing feet of Chuga before washing away.

Chuga, energized by the returning tide, tried to wiggle his way to the water but found himself stuck in the shallow hole he'd developed underneath his body. He would have to wait a little longer for the water, and hope it reached him and could lift him up in its grasp.

Once again Jenuga instructed Chuga to save his energy till the water reached him. He nodded his response and focused on the steady stream of waves as they marched towards him.

25

Barruga watched from the rocks and ice as each wave passed him and continued on, eventually surrendering itself to the shore. One by one they came, each different from the last. Most still came up short, but a special few would splash cool water onto Chuga's face. Just when Barruga was beginning to believe Chuga was going to make it, his breath caught in his throat. Something had moved on the horizon. He'd seen it out of the corner of his eye. He stared at the horizon till his eyes watered. He didn't want to believe it. The light glistened off the snowy shield of land. He blinked his eyes and there it was again. The slightest of movement, but unmistakable.

Barruga stared hard at the spot till he couldn't lie to himself anymore. There was no doubt. As small as it was, bouncing along the dunes, it could only be one thing. The White Beast!

It can't end this way! Barruga thought as his anger welled up inside him. He searched out Chuga on the beach and measured the waves, hoping they wouldn't be too late. As he listened to the hope-filled joy of the pod as they cheered each passing wave to new heights, he watched the slow, steady progress of the approaching doom. There was no mistaking the White Beast now. As it drew ever closer it would stop and sniff the air, pinpoint the smell that drove it, and continue on its way. Chuga was running out of time!

Barruga was torn with whether to warn the others or not. He was still not ready to make himself known. He knew something they didn't, but he wasn't sure it was news they wanted to hear. Especially from him. It was going to be close. As he wrestled with the decision to come forward, fate found a way to make it for him.

When the seabirds saw the White Beast from their lofty vantage point, high on the wind, they cried to each other knowing he would bring an end to their long wait.

Finuga was still watching over the pod from a good distance back when she was attracted to the commotion of the seabirds above. She looked up briefly, and while returning her gaze to the beach, she too saw the unmistakable movement on the horizon. The White Beast!

She didn't know she wasn't the first to see it, and let out a gasp before she could stop herself. It drew the attention of a few adults nearby. When they turned to see what she was staring at, they gasped at what they saw! Not too far away and coming fast was their worst nightmare! The White Beast had arrived!

Word spread like a tsunami and soon even Chuga was aware of the new danger although he couldn't see it himself. He watched their faces as their eyes darted back and forth between him and the approaching danger. He saw the fear grip them and heard it in their frantic voices as they pleaded with him to move.

Jenuga saw the White Beast and her heart sank. He was too close. It would only be moments before it reached the beach, and then Chuga. The waves were not strong enough yet. They needed more time! She told Chuga to get ready. "You mustn't give up, baby," she said with her 'do it now' voice. "It's got to be the next good size wave. You'll need to wiggle and squirm and fight for all you're worth!"

"Okay, Mama," he said with a determination that filled her with pride. He would not let her down. He would never give up! *You'll see Mama,* he thought and focused on the sound of her voice.

"Get ready now, baby," she said.

26

The White Beast reached the top of the last dune and stopped. He gazed upon the fertile sea before him as the seabirds danced and screamed on the winds above. Only a short distance ahead, he scanned the shore of the Black Pebbled Beach for the prize meal that flooded his snout with its delicious scent. When his eyes finally locked onto the small white whale his immediate reaction was disappointment. It was very small compared to the hundreds upon hundreds he saw bobbing in the rising waters of the large inlet. He shook off his discontent and acknowledged the fact that right now any meal – however small – was welcomed, and his luck was such that no other polar bears had already arrived to claim it.

He clambered down the final dune and raced along the water's edge straight for the little white whale. He scrambled around the incoming waves as the seabirds skirted from his path. With just a few hundred yards to go his hunger churned his stomach and his mouth watered. With his eyes on the prize, he did not see the large wave of the incoming tide as it crashed into him and knocked him from his feet.

27

When the next wave hit, Chuga was ready. It crashed before him and sprayed him with foam, but not much water.

"Now!," yelled Mama!

Chuga wiggled and squirmed and fought as hard as he could, but the water barely reached his flippers and receded. He stopped flailing about and waited for the next wave. The next one splashed up around him as he squirmed and kicked. He felt it momentarily lift him from his perch. It was still not enough. He was losing strength fast, but his efforts were not in vain. He managed to free himself from the nest he'd dug, and now rested on the pebbles at its front lip. As he drew up his energy for a last try, he saw a flash of white to his left.

He hesitated for a second and glanced down the shore. What he saw next amazed him.

Barruga's anger had grown to a white-hot fury! The White Beast had crested the last dune, hesitated long enough to spot his quarry, and was now sprinting the last few hundred yards down the beach, straight for Chuga! The last couple of swells had felt weak as they passed him, and Barruga knew they could never reach Chuga in time. In a moment of pure insanity, driven by his rage, Barruga leaped from his hiding spot and propelled himself with all his strength straight at the White Beast! Fueled by his anger, he plowed through the water, adjusting his charge as he went. As he hurtled toward the beach, he began to rise with the swell of a growing wave. As the wave grew, it pulled Barruga up with it, and just like Chuga the day before, it lifted him to its peak and carried him high atop its massive curl.

Jenuga and Annie were urgently pleading for Chuga to fight! He was out of time. The White Beast was almost upon him! When he failed to attempt an escape as the water reached him once again, they turned to follow his gaze.

Chuga blinked the water from his eyes and stared. The White Beast was fast approaching, but that was not the white flash that got his attention. It was Barruga, and he was flying! There he was, high atop a mighty wave, streaking toward the beach and the White Beast!

All the eyes of the pod were now on Barruga as he flew past them in a blur.

For only the second time they witnessed a fellow white whale flying like the birds in the sky. Not knowing whether to cheer or scream, their cries were a confused mass of shock and awe.

Barruga felt the waters resistance leave his charge. He felt the water cascade from his back and the wind sweep past his face. He was flying, but failed to notice. He was caught atop a growing wave and was now at its mercy as it continued on its path to the shore.

Unable to do anything but ride along, Barruga searched for his target. In an instant, he knew he would be too late, as the White Beast raced beyond the spot where he knew he'd land. When he tried to turn the curl of the wave caught him and tumbled him down in a spectacular crash of flying water and white foam that left him in a dazed heap on the pebbled beach.

The massive wave continued its thunderous course along the beach and knocked the unsuspecting White Beast off his feet.

Jenuga, Annie, and the rest of the pod were transfixed by the drama playing out before them. They stared with mouths agape.

Chuga stared down the beach and still couldn't believe what he was seeing. He watched Barruga and the White Beast struggle to right themselves. He had no idea where Barruga had come from, or what he was doing. Chuga was too startled to move!

The White Beast tumbled in the crash of the massive wave, then climbed to his feet as the wash raced back into the sea. He shook the pain from his battered frame and took a deep breath to clear his head. He'd been turned around and now found himself facing a new larger white whale. He was confused. Suddenly they were everywhere, and he didn't know what to think. He'd heard stories of them throwing themselves on the beach, but hadn't believed them. He stared at the new white whale and saw the anger and hate in its eyes.

Barruga stared back at the White Beast and saw confusion and hunger in its eyes. He glanced beyond the White Beast and saw the residue of the large wave swirl around Chuga and race back into itself. *Why didn't he move!* Barruga thought as he turned his attention back to the White Beast.

The White Beast stood still as he puzzled over this second white whale. He turned to look down the beach and saw his original prize staring back from more than a hundred yards away. It was so small. He turned back to the larger prize only fifty feet away and saw the quick movements of a whale not ready to be caught.

Barruga sprang into action when the White Beast looked down the beach at Chuga. He pulled himself through the disappearing wash and bogged down in the empty space where the water had cleared. He was sure to reach safety as the next wave filled the empty space he occupied.

The White Beast, upon seeing the large whale slipping away, covered the ground in a few leaping bounds and flung himself at the vanishing prize.

Chuga and the speechless pod gasped in unison! He again blinked the water from his eyes as the wave that could've freed him washed over and around him seemingly unnoticed. He craned his neck, lifting his head high so he could see over the swirling water around him. He watched the beast pounce on Barruga's back and sink his large claws deep into Barruga's exposed tailfin just before he could duck under the next curl and escape.

Barruga felt the sharp claws as they tore into his tailfin. He felt the awesome strength of the beast as it tried to pull him away from the safety of the water.

The White Beast clung to Barruga with his powerful paws as Barruga fought for his life! Wave after wave pounded them as they wrestled in the crashing surf! As each wave hit, it pushed them back up the shore, giving the beast his footing. Then the rushing water pulled them back to the sea, giving Barruga the means to fight and squirm towards deeper water. Each gained ground only to lose it again in the desperate struggle.

The White Beast knew if he could get the white whale onto the beach, he could have his meal. He doubled his efforts, pulling and dragging with all his strength.

Barruga knew if he didn't reach the safety of the water, he would indeed become a meal! He slashed his tailfin in the shallow wash, trying to dislodge the beast.

Chuga and the rest of the pod watched motionless as back and forth they went through the steady stream of waves the high tide continued to throw at them.

The seabirds screamed in delight as they circled above. Their screams nearly drowned out by the deafening noise of the crashing waves as the tide reached its peak.

And then the sea once again gathered up its might and displayed its force. It pulled the water from the beach into a thundering curl, dragging Barruga and the White Beast helplessly along.

The White Beast hung on with the last of his strength, and dug his hind legs into the ground as he watched the wave reach its peak before him. Unable to move, and unwilling to let go, he took the full force of the massive wave square in the chest. His claws tore through the last length of the whale's tailfin in a desperate bid to hang on, before being wrenched away. As he tumbled back, his flailing limbs searched but found nothing but air. He washed onto the shore in a jumbled heap of exploding water and white foam!

Barruga ducked his head under the curl and fought with his last remaining ounce of strength. He felt the wave pound his back and the painful tear of the beast's claws, and suddenly he was free! He did not hesitate. With a few thrusts of his ravaged tailfin, he propelled himself into the safety of the water. He raced from the beach, not slowing down or turning back, until he neared the mouth of the inlet. He turned and watched the White Beast stare after him. He saw the blood trail in his wake and darted into the safety of his flooded hiding place among the rocks and ice.

The White Beast was stunned by the wallop of the great wave and could not give chase. As his head slowly cleared, he watched the white whale disappear through the surf and escape. He looked at his paws in disbelief and saw the blood and water drip from them. His failure to land the white whale overwhelmed him and he hung his head in defeat. His stomach rumbled and growled at him. Something tugged at his mind, but he could not find its source.

28

C huga was in shock! He had not moved except to fight the water that pulled at him so he could watch the battle unfold.

Jenuga, Annie, and the rest of the pod involuntarily slid back from the beach and away from the stunned White Beast. They too were in shock at what they saw.

Everyone except Barruga momentarily forgot about Chuga. He glanced at the beach and was alarmed to see Chuga still sitting on the shore. He yelled Chuga's name as loud as he could, and it seemed to snap everyone back to the here and now.

The sudden commotion beyond the waves shook the White Beast from his sullen defeat. He looked out across the inlet at the mass of white whales. Their focus was not centered on him and he turned to follow their attention. As he turned, he remembered the original small white whale that had lured him here to begin with. He snapped his head the last few inches and saw with horror the little white whale surrounded in a pool of water left by the previous wave. Without another thought, he leaped to his feet and chased down the beach.

Barruga watched the White Beast turn toward Chuga. He saw the realization on his face that he was about to lose this meal also. Chuga was in the wash, and if he would just move, he would be safe!

Chuga was still stunned by the struggle he witnessed and locked eyes with the White Beast. He'd never seen one before today, and was hypnotized by its gaze.

When the White Beast sprang forward the pod sucked in their breath in unison, then let it out in a variety of screams that mostly meant for Chuga to get his tailfin moving!

Chuga came to life with the sudden movement of the White Beast and kicked and wiggled and squirmed his way through the wash of the receding wave. He made good progress, but was still short of reaching the deeper water when the wave fully departed. Left high and dry once again, he silently urged the next wave to come.

The White Beast, thinking he'd lost even this small prize, found a surge of strength when the wave disappeared while leaving the small white whale behind. He raced along, still dumbfounded at what was happening. He watched the next wave splash around the small whale and hoped it was too weak to propel itself into the deeper water. If it could, he knew he had no chance. He was still too far away. He watched helplessly as the wave returned to the sea leaving an empty beach behind.

Chuga waited until the wave had fully washed over him and then used his renewed energy to drive himself back into the deeper water.

Jenuga, Annie, Barruga, and all the white whales in the inlet, watched with great joy as Chuga seemed to effortlessly slip into the dark water and away from the pebbled beach.

29

The White Beast gathered himself up with all his force and threw himself at the empty space that once held his promised meal captive. Unwilling to give up so easily again, he made a last desperate dive into the surf and popped up swimming. Pulling with his strong paws, he chased the little white whale into the inlet, knowing he had little chance of catching him. He swam in a large arc digging for the nearest whales, who easily retreated to safe distances, hurriedly maneuvering well out of his reach. He finally paused, tiring from his efforts and lack of success, reluctantly succumbed, and dejectedly returned to the pebbled beach. He dragged himself to dry land, violently shook the water from his hide, and sat down hard on his haunches. A wave of nausea swept over him. His empty stomach growled angrily, and his last ounces of energy drained from his body. He collapsed to the ground with a sickening thud and lay there unmoving. Only his eyes flickered while he looked out across the inlet, watching over the pounding surf as the white whales welcomed the small whale back into their fold. He was still confused by what had happened. He tiredly waited for the next white whale to throw itself on the beach. He wanted to be ready. He waited and watched, but they never came.

The seabirds screamed their discontent from high on the wind when they knew no meal was forthcoming. They circled for a while, ever watchful, before giving up hope and returning to the wide-open sea. They carried their disappointment with them as they went in search of their next meal.

30

Chuga easily evaded the White Beast and darted to his Mama's side. Mama guided him in and lifted him onto her back to support his weakened body. With no time to celebrate, she carried him amongst the frightened pod as they scurried away from the clumsy reach of the White Beast. Once safely out of reach, they collectively turned to warily monitor him, prepared to flee again if he persisted. There was a general sigh of relief when they saw him give up and return to the shore.

The entire pod gathered around Jenuga and Chuga and showered them with rousing cheers of heartfelt joy. Jenuga pleaded with them to leave some room so Chuga could catch his breath. While they eased back, she quickly inspected him from head to tailfin, assessing the damages. Unable to find any permanent damage, she gathered him up in her flippers and held him tight.

Chuga was thrilled to be back in the water and safely in his mother's flippers. He was too weak to show his delight and allowed himself to be held close while sharing the joy of the pod with a tired smile. He listened to them chant his name in celebration. "I'm so sorry, Mama," he repeated over and over as she cooed and reassured him. The chanting reminded him of the chants of the day before and the series of events that led to this happy moment. "Where's Barruga," he asked in a worn out voice.

A scowl swept through the pod at the mention of the name.

Barruga hid in the rocks and ice and watched the drama reach its victorious conclusion. He was thrilled to see Chuga join his mother and the rest of the white whales. With his own future uncertain, he hesitated to run away forever, now that he knew all were safe. He listened to the chants and celebration of the pod, while agonizing over his own lonely fate. He wished he could go back and make amends. He would change his ways and be a friend rather than the bully he used to be. But it was too late, and as he turned to flee forever, he was slowed by the quieting of the pod to a hushed silence. He strained to hear as the weak familiar voice of Chuga reached him, and he heard his name. Stopped in his tracks, he listened intently while the pod adamantly protested the sound of his name. But he heard Chuga cry out in protest, "But he saved my life! And he's hurt! We have to find him!"

A groan trickled through the pod as the truth of Chuga's pleas began to sink in. They were not ready to forgive the source of all their recent grief.

"He's right!" Annie chimed in, mimicking Jenuga's 'do it now' voice. "Chuga's right! Barruga risked his life to help Chuga and now he's hurt and needs our help! We must find him fast!"

"Yes," agreed Jenuga. "We're all responsible for what happened." While she continued to speak she slowly turned in a circle, looking as many as she could in the eye and daring them to disagree. "We're all part of a family that helps each other in times of need. Barruga saved Chuga's life! He kept the White Beast busy so Chuga could escape! He put his own life in danger, and now he's hurt and needs our help. We have to find him."

The rest of the pod slowly released their long grown anger, recognizing the truth in Jenuga's pleas. They nodded their agreement and fanned out to begin the search.

It didn't take long before Sandy and Bella found Barruga among the rocks and ice, but they were unable to coax him from his hiding spot. Not knowing what to do, Sandy sent Bella back to the group to fetch Annie for advice.

Bella pulled Annie to the side and quietly said, "We found him, but he won't come out."

"Where is he?" Annie asked.

"Follow me," said Bella. She led Annie to the rocks and ice where Sandy awaited.

"He's in there," said Sandy, pointing to an opening between the rocks.

"Okay," said Annie, "wait here. I'll be back in a minute."

Annie slid between the rocks into the small pool and face to face with Barruga. She could see the pain on his face. The exhaustion and physical pain was obvious. But there was more. He looked lost, scared.

"Let me look at you," said Annie as she circled him slowly. "You're all torn up. Let's get you out of here and get you fixed up." She looked at Barruga expectantly as she drifted to the opening. Barruga hesitated.

"Look," said Annie in a soft tender tone, "you're hurt. You need help. Let us help you."

"But..." said Barruga.

"But what?"

"It was all my fault!" Barruga cried as he hung his head in shame.

"No," said Annie, "it was all our fault. You didn't chase him onto the beach, did you?"

"No, but...?"

"You didn't run away when he needed our help, did you?"

"No."

"And you did the bravest thing anyone could do to try to save him. Did you see anyone else risking their life like you did?"

"No, but..."

"No, but nothing. It's all over, and everyone is okay. Except you. You need our help." She swam up close, resting a comforting flipper upon his back. "Everything is going to be all right. All is forgiven. We're family, and we help each other when needed. We're all trying to do the best we can, but we need to do it together. So, come on. Everyone is waiting for us."

Annie turned and headed toward the opening. This time Barruga didn't hesitate. He followed along dutifully. He was tired, hurt, and lost. There was no fight left in him. He could feel the sting of his damaged tailfin as the rush of adrenaline slowly melted away. He was happy to be told what to do, and happy to oblige. But mostly, he was happy that Annie had come to find him, to rescue him, to be his friend.

They got a warm welcome from Sandy and Bella when they exited the rocks and ice before Bella raced ahead to spread the good news. They could hear the cheers growing as Annie and Sandy led Barruga into the inlet and the crowd of awaiting white whales.

Barruga allowed himself to be guided into the inner circle, where everyone crowded around him. He was face to face with Chuga, Annie, and Jenuga, too stunned to protest or flee. He watched Chuga gather up his returning strength and jumped in fright when Chuga leaped at him and tried to hug him in his small flippers. "Thank you for saving my life!" he heard Chuga whisper. A wave of relief swept over him, and he knew it would be all right.

31

"I'm so sorry," Barruga told Chuga. "I don't want to be a bully anymore. But no one will be my friend," he sobbed, his grief spilling over.

"I will be your friend," said Chuga, and a new cheer rang out through the masses. "Will you promise to be nice from now on?"

"Yes, I promise," Barruga said, and everyone could see he meant it.

"Then, will you be my friend?" asked Chuga.

"Okay," was all Barruga could say, and he gushed with pride. He knew that from this day forth he would never leave Chuga's side. They would be friends forever. He would protect Chuga and all his friends from ever being bullied again by anyone. "I'll be your friend forever!" he said, and another cheer sprang up.

"Then can I call you Barry?" Chuga asked.

"Barry??" said Barruga, "Barry? Really?" No one had ever called him anything but Barruga before, and not always in the nicest tone. Most times it sounded more like a bad word than a good name. Barry sounded like one of the guys. Like the name of a friend. With a tear in his eyes he looked at Chuga to see if he meant it, and found nothing but love and compassion, even a plea for acceptance in Chuga's eyes.

"Yes," said Barruga, "Barry... I like it! Yes, you can call me Barry! And I promise I'll never call you anything but Chuga. No more name calling."

"Good," said Chuga. "Then that settles it." He reached to embrace Barry, but was swallowed up by the much larger friend's hug.

"Three cheers for Barry!" shouted Annie. "Flip, flip hurray!"

Everyone quickly took up the chant, "Flip, flip hurray. Flip, flip hurray!" they cheered most enthusiastically.

"You know," said Chuga slyly, "us flying Belugas have to stick together," and he laughed when he saw the realization flood Barry's face.

The whole pod soon understood what Chuga meant. Though they hadn't thought of it before, they remembered how Barry had caught and ridden a monster wave in his attempt to rescue Chuga. Both of them had flown through the air atop the waves! The chatter rose to new levels as they all relived both the amazing flights, and shared with one another their thoughts.

"What were you thinking, Barry?" asked Chuga.

"I don't know," said Barry, "I just wanted him to stop." They glanced at the beach and saw the White Beast collapsed on the land. "I didn't really have a plan."

"Well, no more wave riding," said Annie in her new 'do it now' voice. She was proud of Barruga. No, Barry. He'd done the right thing, and there was nothing left to say.

Jenuga smiled to herself while holding her tongue. Annie had said what she was thinking, and she was impressed by her maturity.

"No more." agreed Chuga and Barry in unison, then laughed at themselves.

"I mean it!" Annie said, liking the new authority in her own voice.

"We promise!" they said weakly, and there was no laughter to follow. They looked at each other and understood in that moment that Annie was no one to be trifled with. They looked at Annie meekly, hoping to appease her.

"Okay," she said, "that's better." She held their stare for an agonizing second before cracking up and motioning them into her awaiting embrace. They eagerly complied and new cheers of relief and joy erupted.

32

Finuga took Barry aside, and with Annie and Sandy's help, tended to his wounds.

Mama put a flipper around Chuga and said in a tender tone, "That was very nice, baby. I think you made a new friend today, and you may have saved *his* life too." Mama added with pride, knowing how easily Barry would've been hunted down with the blood that flowed from his tailfin. "But you know I almost lost you today."

"I know Mama, I'm so sorry."

"You know when I tell you to do something, or not to do another, it's not to punish you. It's for your own protection. I was so scared, baby. Please don't ever do that again."

"I won't, Mama," Chuga said. "I'm so sorry. I was so scared too. I promise I'll be good and do whatever you say."

"Okay," Mama said, "I guess that was lesson enough for all of us." She knew he would not be able to keep that promise as he continued to grow up. It was alright. She knew he meant it, but he would also grow into his own. She only hoped she could protect him and keep him safe. She knew everyone would remember this day, and hoped its lesson would live on as long as the stories most likely would.

33

The pod slowly left the inlet later that evening as the dusk settled in. After cautiously watching the White Beast prowl the shore for a while, they decided it was best to leave. Their time at the Black Pebbled Beach had pretty much reached its end anyway, and there was no need to risk any further danger posed by the White Beast. When they were sure the Black Beasts weren't lying in wait, they made their way to the open sea. They said their goodbyes and broke off into their own groups to return to their home waters. They carried with them the stories they would tell for generations to come. They would retell over and over the heroic tale of the two white whales who flew through the air like the birds in the sky. They'd retell the close calls of the days, embellishing on the stories as they grew to impossible feats.

Soon it would become a legend that more and more claimed to have witnessed, even though some who told the tales had yet been born.

Barry refused to leave Chuga's side. Kruga, Finuga and the rest of their small pod welcomed him into their growing numbers.

Chuga, Annie, and Barry would become inseparable friends and live long, adventurous lives together. They would return year after year to the Black Pebbled Beach, and be greeted by a hero's welcome.

Jenuga and Finuga watched them grow through the years to follow, and their families grow around them.

And Chuga would one day see Lilly again. But that's another story.

34

On a lonely black pebbled beach in the cold north, the White Beast gazed across the empty sea. Sitting on his haunches, he looked around the vast horizon and saw no discernible signs of life. The white whales were gone. The seabirds had vacated the sky above. The once fresh scent of a promised meal had drifted away on the ocean's steady breeze. He could feel the emptiness in the air, and bowed his head in despair. He slowly, reluctantly, lifted his weary weight to his feet. With a last longing look at the sea, he turned and walked away, carrying his hunger with him.

the end

About the Author:

Carl F. Kristeller writes from his home in the suburbs of Syracuse, NY.

About the Illustrator:

Joshua Anthony Sacco is the owner and operator of Reflective Design, located in Camillus, NY. He specializes in conceptual design.

You can visit chugathebeluga.com to learn more.

Made in the USA
Middletown, DE
30 June 2015